NO ONE IN A WHEELCHAIR CAN GET IN HERE!

Samantha saw that sign first because it was impossible not to see, with its big blue lettering and large white background. The other signs propped up against the wall were printed in bold black and red. One of the signs was being held by a boy in a wheelchair.

If Samantha could have run from the spot, she would have. But she couldn't go anywhere. The crowd around her had her wedged tightly and for an endless moment all she could think of was that now they knew, all of them around her. They knew, as certainly as she knew it, that she was unable to use the girl's room.

Samantha finally managed to turn her chair around and was about to leave when she froze to the sound of an arrogant voice behind her.

"Hey, you, you in the wheelchair. Don't leave. Come on up here and help me out . . ."

Run, Don't Walk

A Novel by
Harriet May Savitz

A SIGNET VISTA BOOK

NEW AMERICAN LIBRARY

NAL BOOKS ARE AVAILABLE AT QUANTITY DISCOUNTS
WHEN USED TO PROMOTE PRODUCTS OR SERVICES. FOR
INFORMATION PLEASE WRITE TO PREMIUM MARKETING
DIVISION, NEW AMERICAN LIBRARY, 1633 BROADWAY,
NEW YORK, NEW YORK 10019.

RL 5/IL 6+

SIGNET, SIGNET CLASSIC, MENTOR, PLUME, MERIDIAN AND NAL
BOOKS are published by New American Library,
1633 Broadway, New York, New York 10019

FIRST SIGNET PRINTING, SEPTEMBER, 1980

6   7   8   9   10   11   12   13   14

PRINTED IN CANADA

PUBLISHER'S NOTE

**To Four Remarkable Women
Who Honor Me
With Their Friendship
And Their Trust . . .**

Nancy Silovitz Greenbaum

Linda Hadley Hoffman

Arlene Kohl Silverstein

Jeanne Galitz Trulick

Run Don't Walk

1 ————

The golden retriever had no business looking at her that way, with her nose thrust toward her, and her eyes warm, hoping. Samantha Lee Anderson looked away. She wheeled over to another cage, her blue eyes already searching anxiously for her mother.

Sam hated coming to this animal shelter, with its cages and animals spilling from them. If her mother hadn't needed help in carrying the cookie boxes for their yearly bazaar, she wouldn't have come at all.

A helplessness always spread over her when she came here to the animal shelter, even though she could think of no better place to put lost or unwanted animals. Still, the feeling of confinement reached out from the iron bars and caught her.

A cocker spaniel playfully jumped around his

kennel, putting on an impromtu performance for Samantha. "I'm not here to take you home, so save your energy," she advised the excited dog. Still, she couldn't help smiling back at the dog's wagging tail.

Even as Sam wheeled toward the other end of the corridor, she sensed the eyes of the golden retriever following her from cage to cage. Samantha felt as if the dog had set a claim on her, as if there were no others in the room but she and the retriever.

Her mother's voice drifted in from the front office. "I do hope your bazaar is a success. You're doing such a fine job here."

They were. They fed and housed so many unwanted animals who would have wandered the wintry city streets, hungry, dodging traffic, sometimes even joining packs and growing mean through necessity. And yet, Samantha could never forget the small room at the other end of the building, the one nobody spoke about. She always thought about it when she came here, though she tried to convince herself that all of the animals would be adopted. She knew they wouldn't be, or couldn't be, and then would come the small room at the other side of the building that snuffed out life. She didn't know a better way to deal with that, either.

Suddenly, she had a desperate need to get away from the loving eyes and wet tongues that licked her fingers.

She knew she would have to pass the golden retriever again to rejoin her mother. "I'll go right past you," she murmured huffily, not daring to look to the side where the warm brown eyes were waiting.

Samantha spun the wheels of her wheelchair faster, tossing her long black hair out of the way as she approached the doorway. But she didn't quite make it. Instead, as if obeying a silent command, her wheels stopped spinning and came to a halt in front of the retriever's cage.

Samantha looked up, defeated. The dog sat there, golden, with sprays of red and brown running through her fur. She sat quietly, not panting, nor asleep in a corner, but with a rare majesty about her. She held her head so high, this proud hunting dog, certainly higher than any other dog in the kennel. Her paws, large and lightly golden, moved their way slowly, cautiously, up and down the bars of the cage.

Samantha sat there, feeling as if she were in a tug-of-war, one which she was quickly losing.

She wheeled closer to the cage until her feet were touching the bars. She wouldn't have known this but for the fact that she saw it. The sense of feeling was gone from her legs, gone as quickly as seashells scooped up by the incoming tide.

The sensation in her legs had been there, once, over a year ago, back in her senior year of high school. Then had come a summer day when she had run to the lake. She had come home from the lake that day feeling nothing from the waist down.

A cold wet nose brought her abruptly back to the present. The retriever had squeezed its nose through the bars and was licking her hand which lay up against the cage.

"Oh, I see you've met Mandy." The woman from the front office was now standing by Samantha's side. Sam's mother walked behind her, her small, slim figure almost hidden by the woman in front of her.

The cool soft nose still pressed against Sam's hand.

"She's so affectionate," Samantha said softly. The dog now shoved her head under Sam's open palm, waiting to be stroked.

"Sam, we really have to get back home." Her mother gently pushed the wheelchair away from the cage. Usually, if someone pushed her wheelchair in a direction she might not have cared to take, Sam would just let the wheels go that way. Somehow, this past year, it didn't seem to matter which way she went. One road was as good as another.

Today, for the first time in a long while, she put on her brakes in defiance.

"Was she lost?" she asked, looking back at the large eyes that seemed to be saying something to her. Sam stared deep into Mandy's wide-eyed stare, hoping she might understand the message. She felt her mother's impatient fingers tapping on the back of her wheelchair.

"No," the woman's face softened. "Mandy is a year old. Her master was a hunter. He took her out one day to try her in the woods when he went to hunt. He discovered she was afraid of noise. The sound of the shotgun terrorized her. So," the woman shrugged helplessly, "he brought her in to us."

"Honey," Samantha felt her mother's hand on her shoulder, "Dad will be home soon. I don't want him to have to wait for dinner."

Samantha nodded. She knew how her mother worried. After the heart attack that had temporarily struck her father down, he had to watch his diet, not gulping big portions of food as he once had, giving up his cigarettes. The only thing that had remained the same in her father's life was his job as driver of the school bus. And fetching, as he often did for Sam.

It was the thought of his constantly running on small errands for her that kept her brakes locked. "What's going to happen to her?" she persisted.

The woman's eyes, once bright and animated, darkened. Her voice hedged, trying to detour around the truth. "She's been here about a month now. Usually dogs like Mandy are adopted right away. Some are trained for the blind, and some for those in wheelchairs. You know, to carry things. They're really quite good at fetching, books and eyeglasses, even something as fragile as a tissue. The golden retriever is quite an intelligent dog," she boasted. "But with Mandy," she hesitated, "it's her fear of noise that discourages everyone from adopting her. She would never do well in traffic, with horns honking."

Samantha looked up at the woman. They both felt the echo of the small room hidden in the back, the room where dogs went to die when adoption possibilities had ceased.

Samantha now understood the message in the dog's eyes. "Take me out of this cage." Mandy's plea was reaching her. She could feel it in her hands when the dog licked her fingers.

Samantha's blue eyes fought to hold back the tears. She hadn't cried . . . not after the dive off the dock, not in the hospital, not when the wheelchair was first brought to her, not even when she knew it was for good. She quickly wiped the wet drops away and unlocked her brakes. The dog made her feel vulnerable; had cut into her self-control without warning. She didn't like the feeling. Samantha sensed her mother's relief as she wheeled toward the exit.

She let herself be guided through the narrow doorway, past the front office with its volunteers busily checking files, down the long slope of the hill that served as parking for the animal shelter.

Sam's mother opened the front door of the car. With her brother Bucky away at school, Sam realized it was now usually just the two of them . . . Sam transferring to the front passenger seat of the car, her mother folding the wheelchair neatly and slipping it in the back . . . first removing the foot pedals and cushion, just as easily as one might remove first hat, then coat when entering a house. The habit had become a ritual, the ritual a habit. They had done it so many times together that it seemed everyone must enter a car that way. But they knew everyone didn't.

They both tried to keep Sam's father out of it as much as possible. The heart attack had left him with a scar, a weakness that came over him suddenly, even though he automatically ran to Sam's aid when she needed help.

The biggest crisis had been his job. They were thankful that the school board saw him fit to still drive the school bus. But he had to be careful. It was always there. His need of quiet, peaceful moments and the wheelchair that demanded physical strength.

Samantha sat by the open car door, her thoughts racing back to the golden retriever. Once, last year, a woman had come to the rehabilitation unit to speak of dogs that could fetch pocketbooks, even crutches. She had stressed the fact that they often acted like an extra set of legs. Sam thought again of her father, of the many times she called, "Dad, I forgot . . ." and then he would get up, even though, sometimes, he had been in the middle of a nap, and look around for the thing she needed and which remained out of reach in another area of the house. But a dog, a dog who could fetch: an extra set of legs.

Mandy could be taught. Sam just knew it. The dog's eyes were brimming with intelligence, pleading for the chance to try.

Sam's mother stood there patiently, waiting for her to transfer. The cool, late summer breeze slipped through Sam's dark hair and scattered it across her striped jersey. Yet, she didn't move. She heard her mother ask, "Sam, are you all right?"

She nodded. School would be starting in a couple of weeks. It would be her first time back since the "dip into the lake." One year ago her class had graduated, and now all new faces would be waiting for her at Scot High.

Mandy's alert eyes came back to her. What if she could teach the dog to carry her books, to bring her things in the house instead of having to call, "Dad, I forgot my sweater on the couch." or, "Mom, did I leave the book in the dining room?" How she hated that, more than anything, the asking of little things. If Bucky had been there, it would have been different. For the past year, he had run for her and done her errands. But he was off to college now, in Colorado, skiing down the slopes.

The car door still swung open, like a beckoning hand.

"Sam . . ." Her mother's voice was worried now. "What is it, honey. Are you ill?" She bent down, facing Samantha, looking at her with the same worried expression that so often crossed her face lately.

Sam wasn't sure if she was ill or not. The high cheekbones tightened beneath the pale blue eyes. She knew she couldn't leave Mandy behind in the cage.

Samantha turned her wheelchair around abruptly so that it was facing the hill and the animal shelter. The wheelchair seemed to capture her look of defiance.

"Mom, I've got to go back and get the dog. Mandy."

"What?" And then after a moment of thoughtful silence: "We can't take care of a dog. Especially that one. She's so big!"

Samantha shook her head stubbornly and the soft waves of her hair tumbled about. "I'll train her. You'll see. She'll fetch for me and make it so much easier for all of us. Dad and you won't have to keep bringing me the things I forget to take with me. You know how I'm always leaving my glasses, or a sweater, or something in the room I've just left." Her mouth was set, as if the discussion had already taken place and ended, the decision now firm.

"But who will take care of her? Who will walk her?"

"I will."

How? The word wasn't spoken. It just hung there like a sword. Samantha felt as if she were sitting under it.

"If I can't," Sam pleaded, "we'll give her back." She had no intention of ever doing that, but it seemed the proper thing to say at this particular time. "Mom, I just can't leave without her." Samantha felt her throat tighten as it always did when she was ready to cry. She didn't want to cry now. It seemed unfair to win that way.

Her mother shook her head, slammed the car door in one of the few fits of anger she had ever allowed herself since the accident, and pushed Sam back up the long hill. It was too steep a hill for Sam to have climbed herself, though right now she wished she might have had that strength in her arms.

They paid the few dollars' donation at the front office and filled out the forms. Sam's heart fluttered as they went back down the long corridor of cages. Mandy still sat there, her head turned their way, as if she were waiting, her neck held high, with that same edge of majesty, the paws still rubbing slowly up and down the cage.

One of the helpers opened the cage door. A collar and leash were put on the dog. Mandy walked quietly beside the wheelchair as if she had always been there. Together, they left the shelter.

Sam's eyes closed a moment as the sun splashed across her face. She held tightly to the leash. The large dog slowly followed the pace of the wheels, as if she understood. A surge of newfound confidence swept over Samantha with her first big decision quietly walking next to her.

Samantha and her mother were both unprepared for what happened next. A car backfired. One might almost have thought it was a gun being shot. Sam's mother had her hands tightly on the push handles of the wheelchair, guiding it down the steep slope. Her touch was not prepared for Mandy's lurch forward, long legs picking up to a gallop while Sam held on to the leash, both out of panic and desperation. Samantha and the wheelchair were torn from her mother's grasp.

"Stop! Stop!" Samantha's screams rolled down the blacktop hill as they approached the rush of traffic in the main street.

"Stop! Please, Mandy. Stop!"

Mandy hit the curb with a fierce howl, and then pulled to a sudden stop as if she were a driver suddenly stepping down on the brakes.

Samantha stopped short, too. The sudden jolt of her wheelchair threw her out of the chair and onto the hard surface of the hill.

Above her mother's screams and the flurry of excitement of people running about her, Sam felt Mandy's hot breath over her face, and her warm tongue licking the dirt off her cheeks and eyes. She was cleaning her face as if Sam were Mandy's puppy.

Samantha reached up and touched the dog's russet colors that shone in the sun, and smiled, and then the smile turned into a laugh, and as she laughed, she put her arms around Mandy's neck.

Arms reached out to help her, but for the first time in many dependent months, she waved them away. She wanted to be able to choose her own way of getting out of this mess. At last, with Mandy, she had a choice.

"Come on, girl, go, girl, take me back to the wheelchair, go ahead, straight ahead, Mandy walk ..." Sam coaxed her.

The dog hesitated, then walked a couple of steps, dragging Sam with her.

"Good, good girl, go ahead, keep going." Samantha let herself be pulled as Mandy walked slowly, carefully past those who had come to help, back up the few steps of the hill toward the wheelchair.

"Oh, Mandy, it's going to be good, I know it is. With you by my side at Scot High, it's all going to work out now," she whispered as the dog's strong body led her to where the wheelchair was waiting.

2 ——————

Johnny Jay wheeled into the large room which was on the third floor of City Hall. The building was closed except for the special entrance which allowed him to enter the building and to reach the third floor by elevator. He looked around quickly for a friendly face. Several people clung together in deep conversation in a corner, their hands gesturing in excited conversation. One of the men was in a wheelchair. The other, speaking to a deaf person, was an interpreter. A woman with long blond hair and a bright red dress held tight to the leash of a Seeing Eye dog. A tall girl with wide dark eyes leaned on crutches.

It was the greatest assortment of poses Johnny had ever seen gathered in one room. Some were bent and listening. Others were straight and tall, using sign language. Some were dwarf-like in their size. Most sat in wheelchairs.

It was Johnny's third meeting of NOD (Now Organized Disabled) and yet Johnny felt enclosed, as if the members had been his friends for a long time. From the moment they had met, he felt they were joined in purpose. Today, he had come for their help.

A brightly painted yellow crutch with blue polka dots waved in the air. "Hey, Johnny, over here." Johnny pushed toward the yellow flash still waving over the heads of some of the members already taking their places in preparation for the meeting. The officers wheeled toward the head table.

Jim Muller put down his crutch and put out his hand instead. "Glad you came back, kid." He shook Johnny's hand vigorously. "We need more young ones like you." His eyes widened with excitement. "Should be a great meeting today. We finally got an O.K. on those buses. I think people are finally beginning to believe we mean business."

Johnny moved into the vacant spot next to Jim. He wished he had been around during their battle so that he could share in their victory. The group had fought long and hard with the Department of Transportation. NOD hoped to make all new public buses purchased with Department of Transportation grants designed so that the elderly and handicapped passengers might use them with ease. There had been lawsuits, and now the word was around that the disabled had won. Years of battling, years of protest and demonstrations and meeting upon meeting had paid off. Jim had filled him in on the history of their campaign to get adequate busing. Over a year ago, Johnny Jay remembered seeing pictures of a group of people in wheelchairs, some standing with Seeing Eye dogs, but all picketing the Bus Administration Building. At that time, there were no buses in the city for the disabled to use.

There still weren't. But this group had won the legal battle, and with the courts on their side, they would eventually get their buses.

Waiting. It was just a matter of waiting. Johnny pushed himself up in the wheelchair so that he was almost standing, as he exercised his muscles while preventing pressure sores. The doctors had told him such push-ups could help keep his kidneys clean. He would often do this exercise of pushing, his long strong arms holding his body erect for a moment, then slipping back in the chair. Sometimes it almost looked as if he might walk away. He never did. He wouldn't. He knew that.

He didn't feel like waiting anymore for what he needed. He felt he wanted what was due him now. Johnny had felt that way even when he was a child and no one wanted to play with him because they weren't quite sure how to play with the kid in the wheelchair. The mothers were afraid their children would hurt him. His mother was afraid he would get hurt. So everyone had stayed away.

Once, just for the shock of it, he had slid out of the chair and lain on the ground, just to build a mud castle. Another time, he slid out of his chair to wrestle on the ground with a classmate. Before their fight, the boy had always seen the wheelchair first and Johnny second. Johnny had kept him pinned on the ground that day until the boy realized that Johnny Jay was the one he had to deal with, not the wheelchair.

His mother spent a lot of time walking back and forth to school that year, talking to teachers, explaining John's attitude, though more often than not she left it unexplained.

"Johnny," she would say, as if saying it one more time might make it happen, "you must learn to control your temper. No one will like you if you don't."

He didn't much care about being liked. He cared more about being heard. Everyone around him seemed to feel that if he kept quiet, he was being good. He felt frightened that he would just disappear.

And then while he was wondering if anything would ever change, 504 had been passed, the section of the Rehabilitation Act that had given him equal rights as a disabled person. He hadn't known it before, that he had never been written into the law. As a disabled person, he had lived to his seventeenth year without any rights at all. He couldn't take the rights of the able-bodied as his rights for they didn't fit his needs. Even though he had the right to travel in this free country he lived in, as a disabled person, he couldn't get into the buses or trains. He realized that even though he had the right to an education, he couldn't be guaranteed to be able to get into the schools because of steps. And even though he had the right to work, which sometimes frightened him when he thought about it, he wasn't sure if anyone would hire him.

Without 504 he couldn't have fought it. With the bill, he had a chance. It had given his anger a purpose.

Johnny tapped impatiently on the arm of his chair. "Come on, get the meeting started," he muttered, and his freckles crowded together as they often did when his face grew taut.

"Red, we're on the crest of victory." Jim's big body leaned forward on his crutches. "We've got the law on our side. All we have to do is put teeth into it to make it work."

Johnny looked up and his brown eyes challenged Jim. "That's all?" he asked. And then he added, "That's everything." He wasn't thinking of the buses now. He was thinking of what was facing him tomorrow, of why he had come here for help. He wondered if the law and 504 were enough.

Johnny sat back against the foam rubber pillow he kept as a cushion between his body and the wheelchair, and relaxed. The president of NOD called the meeting to order. A hush swept across the room and there was a momentary scurrying for empty places.

The gavel banged against the desk. The meeting was finally called to order.

The president opened the meeting with a brief speech. "We've come a long way this year." Applause stopped her for a moment. She pushed her long blond hair back off her shoulders and paused letting everyone have their expression of victory. The Seeing Eye dog lay curled up at her feet. "Section 504 opened the door for all of us." Her voice grew stronger, surprisingly loud for one so seemingly small in build. "And when the Department of Transportation announced the decision to require all new public buses purchased with Department of Transportation grants to be designed for easy access by the elderly and handicapped, it was the icing on the cake. These new buses," she took a deep breath, "will have low, step-into bus features, only six inches from the curb. Some buses will be made with special kneeling features that lower buses to the curb."

Her face grew flushed with the possibilities of the future. Johnny felt the inside of his chest tighten, the way it did sometimes before he had a fight with a classmate.

He wanted to do that now. He wanted to wrestle all the changes at once, out on the ground, where he could settle it once and for all, where he could win or lose and go away knowing. But he knew it couldn't be that way. And the tight fist in his chest stayed there . . . waiting.

"One bus from each contractor will be fitted with an optional electrically operated ramp or lift.

The front door of a Transbus will be twenty-five percent wider and more brightly illuminated than the entrances of today's buses." The dream was now spun before Johnny. Buses he actually could get on. On his way to work someday, choosing not to drive his car, or maybe that day it had broken down, there he was with a briefcase in hand, because accountants usually carried briefcases, and the bus would pull up. The steps of the bus would slide down almost like escalator steps and turn into a ramp. Or maybe just like a prince's subject kneeling at his feet. He'd board the bus. Before, buses had always passed him by, with other people's faces staring out the windows. Now, he could see his own face staring out. Ride a bus. Ride a bus. He had never even been in one.

"Wherever we are, we must all now take action in our own communities," the president went on, "to change whatever needs to be changed. Let's forget the bitterness, let's forget what was." And then very quietly, almost as if she were speaking to herself, and Johnny and the others were eavesdroppers, she said, "Today must be the first day of the rest of our lives."

Johnny's fists were now clenched. He waited through the secretary's report, the treasurer's report, the separate committees on housing, on the monthly newsletter, on next month's schedule.

"You're awfully quiet today." Jim leaned toward him and gave him a long look from under his furry eyebrows.

But Johnny barely heard him. All he heard was,

"New business," and then his wheels were in motion, out into the aisle and up in front of the table which housed the officers. He had known ever since he had seen Scot High that a moment such as this would come. The move from the other state had hurt, leaving old friends, the safety of a school that had been familiar with his needs. It had hurt plenty. It had been an old school, a good old school. Oddly enough, it had been accessible: the front doorway was stepless and wide, the bathrooms old-fashioned, almost like a sitting room.

The fresh indignation returned. "Johnny, why don't you come over here and talk from the table?" the president invited him.

Then had come the move, and last week the inspection of his new school, before he was actually to be mainstreamed into its river of walking students. School was to begin tomorrow and he was living with the knowledge and fear of something he knew was impossible to change by then.

All week he had known that he couldn't get into the toilet. He had mentioned it to the principal. The principal had mumbled something about getting the school board to allocate funds for alterations to the toilets, but it might take some time.

Johnny knew the alternative was a special school. That wasn't his idea of mainstreaming. So he had kept quiet. But he knew. And his parents knew. And none of them knew what to do about it, except that he drive home and use the toilet at his own house whenever necessary.

Johnny was now behind the speakers' table with the microphone in his hand. He looked out on an assortment of wheelchairs, crutches, aid dogs, and warm, friendly faces. He cleared his throat and felt the familiar tightening throughout the upper part of his body. He didn't much feel like speaking in front of a group about a problem as personal as this one.

The faces became curious, then questioning as the silence clung to the front of the room.

"Sometimes," his father had said last night when he had told him what he was about to do, "sometimes you have to have help. You just can't do everything yourself, Johnny." Up to that time he had tried.

The words started flowing into the microphone. "I'm a new member here and I need your help." His legs began to spasm and he cursed them. They always picked a time to jump up and down when he least wanted them to. Johnny held them in place for a second until he felt himself relax and his limbs calm down. The people in the audience understood. They waited patiently.

"I'm starting a new school tomorrow. Scot High." He hesitated. His pride in being independent—in not asking for anyone's help—stopped the words from coming out.

"Go ahead, Johnny. Tell us about it," Jim Muller shouted from the back.

"Well," he sorted out his thoughts aloud, "I

don't know too much about the school except," and the anger returned, "I can't get into the toilets."

A unified groan swept through the NOD members. For a moment, Johnny could not speak above the roar of indignation that echoed throughout the room.

"What are you going to do about it, Red?" a short man with dark glasses called out. He sat in the front row, leaning forward on his walking cane.

"You going to let that happen to you, Johnny?" another challenged.

Johnny shrugged, and his wide shoulders hung there in hesitation. They expected something from him, almost like a teacher with the text questions on the blackboard.

"What can I do?" he asked desperately. "I just can't go and knock the toilets down."

A thunderous applause was his answer. The gavel behind him slammed against the large walnut table.

"Come on now. You're not being fair. If you have any suggestions for Johnny, one at a time, let's hear them." The president tried for some order.

A woman with burn scars crisscrossing the edges of her face spoke first. "You're entitled to an education, Johnny, by law. The school also owes you an accessible toilet." Then faster than he could cope with them, came one urgent suggestion after another.

"Get some signs, Johnny. Demand that they

widen the toilet doors and that you have a cubicle that you can get into."

"Picket the toilet. Keep the school's attention on the fact that you can't get into their facilities."

"Write to the office of civil rights."

"Let them know you're there."

"Make some noises, Red. Not violent ones, but the kind of noise that will let them know you care. If you don't care, they won't care."

"But it's only me." Johnny protested. "So what if I carry a sign? What difference would it make?" He threw his doubt back at them.

A man from the front row wheeled up to him. His eyes burned through a thin-boned face. "Because, my boy, you're going to make enough noise and so much of it that they will rip down that door and build a wider doorway that you can get through."

"And if they don't?" Johnny questioned the man as they sat facing each other, wheelchair to wheelchair.

The man drew closer. "You try it that way for a while, kid. And then if that doesn't work," and he put his arm out as if to embrace the group behind him, "well, then, we've got a few more tricks up our sleeve. We won't give up."

Johnny wanted to ask him what he meant by tricks, but the gavel cut his thoughts off as the meeting came to a close.

He didn't stay around to talk as he often did at the end of a meeting. Though many of the members had more encouragement and advice to offer,

Johnny excused himself. He knew what he had to do now. And for the time being, he would have to do it alone.

Johnny stopped at the art shop on the way home. He picked up two large pieces of canvas. He balanced them on his lap up the steep parking lot hill and over the deep red carpets of the apartment house corridor.

His sister Karon opened the door. "Johnny, we've been waiting dinner for you." She enjoyed playing older sister to him, even though she was four years younger. She quickly relieved him of the canvases.

"I had to go to the art shop after the meeting," he apologized. His father was already seated at the table, tossing the salad.

His mother examined the wrapped canvases. "What's this?" she asked.

Johnny stretched over the kitchen sink and washed his hands. He had always taken the direct route with his parents and they with him. When he had become old enough to understand that he would always be in a wheelchair, and that not everyone was born with a spine slightly bent out of shape and two dangling legs, his parents had talked honestly to him about it. When his father had lost his job as an engineer and they had to move to this new state, they had met together in a family conference.

Karon had been reluctant about the change, the parting from old friends. But it was Johnny whom the family conference had centered on. For it was

Johnny who had gone to so many special schools
for so many years because the public schools
wouldn't take him. It was Johnny who finally had
grown to high-school age in a state where there
was an old school that was accessible to his needs.

That had been then. Before the move. They all
had agreed that his father's job must come first.
They had clung together in a circle of support, as
always. He wasn't about to break it now. He knew
he had to level with them.

"You know about the toilets?" he said as he
pulled over to the table. He reminded them of
their suggestion to get a written excuse to go
home whenever necessary. "I brought the problem
up today at the NOD meeting."

"You're going to do something about it?" It was
more of a statement than a question coming from
his father. Johnny nodded. He felt a surge of
power as he saw the look of pride in his father's
eyes.

The rest of the meal went by quietly. No one
asked him what he was going to do. They knew
he'd tell them when he was ready. It was as if they
were all in the same battalion, a small sector of
troops sensing an important siege ahead.

After dinner, Johnny carried the canvases into
his room. He set them flat on the bed and got
some crayons from his desk drawer. For a long
moment he sat there, crayon poised, waiting for
the right words to volunteer and fill up the blank
boards. Then, slowly, the pencil began to move
across the clean canvas, filling it with large, bold

letters. **I don't expect miracles. I just want to be able to use the bathrooms.** He sat back to survey the statement. Then underneath in even bolder print. **Section 504 gave us our civil rights . . . that includes the right to a public education. But it's hard to learn when you have cramps.**

He stood the one sign up against the wall and read it over aloud. He was beginning to feel better. His parents' decision to bring him home to the bathroom had touched him with a sense of defeat. The sign in front of him gave him a small hope of victory. Now, at least with the bright letters staring back at him, he had a sense of power.

He went back to the bed, his fingers moving quickly with excitement. With a bright red pencil, he wrote. **Section 504—no otherwise qualified handicapped individual in the U.S. . . . shall, solely by reason of his handicap, be excluded from the participation in, be denied the benefit of, or be subjected to the discrimination under any program or activity receiving federal financial assistance. (HEW regulation)**

Another sign soon read, **The bill of rights for the handicapped was spelled out in Title V of the Rehabilitation Act of 1973, and we are going to enforce the regulations that are specified in that bill. (President Jimmy Carter)** The printing sped on. **I expect to get those rights. . . . and I am tired of waiting. (Johnny Jay)**

It was late when he finished, yet there was still the low hum of the television set coming from the living room. Johnny wheeled over and opened his bedroom door. His father was the first to come into the room.

"Are you finished?" he asked.

Johnny was surprised to see Karon had been waiting up too.

"Wow!" Karon's blue eyes turned twice their size. "What great colors."

His mother stood there in silence. He saw her shoulders straighten as she read the signs aloud.

For a moment each of them was lost in the meaning of the words. Karon was the first to break the silence.

"Hey, Johnny," she asked, "why would they change those brand-new toilets just for you?"

The question hung there in the room for a long time, no one wanting even to recognize that it existed. Johnny knew there would be many people asking that very same question.

3 ————

Samantha stroked Mandy's long ears, then wheeled through the front doorway of the sprawling high school. "We're here, Mandy," she said, "at last."

Samantha knew now that she couldn't have made this first day back to school without Mandy by her side. From the moment they had joined forces, the dog held a portion of Sam's mind. Sometimes Mandy would just look straight into her eyes to sense her moods, to predict her needs. She gave Sam the chills with her perception. The dark brown eyes would look at her, waiting for the command, the neck straight, the body alert, ready, almost pleading for another job, the tail wagging, thumping against the floor or the chair. Mandy wanted to work. It was if she had been waiting for the jobs Sam assigned her, as though the days of frolicking would have been a bore if there was nothing constructive in between.

Come . . . sit . . . fetch . . . the glasses over there . . . there on the table . . . pointing . . . Mandy watching the finger as if it were an arrow . . . turning to where it pointed. Trying the book . . . no, not that . . . the bag . . . no . . . no . . . there . . . . glasses . . . over and over and then, delicately, between her teeth, as if she held a sparrow which she often might just hold, like a treasure, bringing it to Samantha like a birthday gift, all but tied and wrapped. Over and over, the schoolbag, the shoes at the bottom of the closet, shoes . . . no, Mandy . . . not the stuffed doll, over and over as the mornings came up, only to hold another training session, and the nights found them both curled up in bed, exhausted, having learned another word, having opened another door.

And now the door to school. This was going back, but it really wasn't going back at all. Not the way things were. Many of the familiar faces were gone. There would be a new senior class now and she would be new to them. Going back. She pushed on the rims of the wheelchair and it reminded her that some things were final. Final. Say it. Believe it. Face it and go from there.

At the Rehabilitation Unit, a physical therapist had cautioned her, "Sam, someday you're going to have to take a stand on something. It might be just making your mind up that you're disabled and saying it to yourself until you believe it."

She knew everyone at the unit was convinced that she hadn't accepted the accident at the lake. Never speaking about it. Keeping the facts of that day locked inside, where she kept her self-control neatly stored.

She never again spoke about that day one year ago. It seemed the best way for her to live with it. No one else around her agreed. "You're living in a dream world, Samantha," the therapist had cautioned. "You think all of this is going to change back tomorrow."

It was her dream world. They had no right to destroy it, no right even to enter it. Except for Mandy. She had penetrated Samantha's privacy, yet had not disturbed a thing.

Dreams were the only release she had from the frustrations that reality brought with it. Dreams, and her writing. But now Sam felt the wet cold nose press against her elbow as she paused for a moment, catching her breath against her excitement. And now Mandy.

Mandy made everything real. It was hard to disappear into drifting moments with that cold nose always bringing her back to reality, or the paws finding their way into her lap, or the tongue forever wanting to splash about her face, as if Mandy needed to be reminded that there were love and caring. Perhaps they both needed to be reminded of that.

Today seemed like a dream, too. She had relived the coming back so many times, as if going through it would guarantee her getting it right.

The books took on added weight as she made her way down the long corridor. "Take the books, Mandy," Sam ordered the dog. Mandy took hold of the handle of the schoolbag in her teeth and slid it off Sam's lap. She gripped the bag tightly as they continued their journey, fully involved in her work, not paying too much attention but accepting the pats on her back, the comments of "Good dog. Hey, you're pretty," from students who happened by and kneeled by her side, wanting a moment of Mandy's attention. If she held the spotlight as the most unusual student of the day, she didn't show that she knew.

Samantha was relieved. The spotlight was on Mandy. It left her where she wanted to be. Second. In the shadows.

Though the beginning of their relationship had been an unpredictable one, with Sam's mother threatening Mandy with a swift return to the animal shelter, the furor had calmed down and turned into a training period, where Mandy might have another chance.

From the time Mandy got up in the morning and brought Sam her crutches until the time she folded up sleepily at the foot of Sam's bed, Mandy was a working dog, with respect only for the real, for what she had to do, for the orders that she looked to Sam for, for what she could see and taste and sniff and explore as her nose whiffed at the inner secrets of the ground.

Though they had only been together for a few weeks, Samantha couldn't imagine the day begin-

ning without Mandy's exuberance. At first it had
been Mandy straining at the wheelchair, pulling it
at her pace, taking Sam for the walk. But gradually the situation had reversed as Mandy seemed
to sense she had an important job to do, and that
listening was one of them. Soon Mandy was letting the wheelchair lead her, her gold red body
carefully slowing down when her enthusiasm
caught at her legs and made her forget.

Mandy also seemed to know that she was in a
trial period. It was as if the two of them were hur-
rying toward a deadline, toward the time that had
turned into today, when they were now moving
past the lockers like a team, down the long hall-
ways as if they both had every right to do so,
though Mandy was the only dog in the school, and
Samantha was the only one in a wheelchair.

Sam checked the numbers on the classroom
doors, hesitating here and there to get her bearings.

Mandy kept firm against the rushing about and
pushings of bodies against her. Sometimes she
bumped against the wheelchair, then quickly
pushed away.

The bell rang just as they entered homeroom.
Samantha grabbed hold of Mandy's collar, feeling
the dog's dread as if it were her own.

"It's O.K., girl," she soothed, for it was her turn
now to take care of Mandy's need. "It's just a bell.
It won't hurt you, Mandy. Good girl. You're safe
with me. No guns here, Mandy. No killing. You're
here with me now, Mandy." Her hand stroked the

body that had hardened to stone. Gradually, it softened under her touch, and then the long tail was thumping against the chair.

Samantha sat there in the aisle, facing the desks, each with a chair neatly tucked under it. The teacher saw her indecision. His name was Mr. Luber. He pulled a chair aside in the front row to make room for her wheelchair.

"Give me the schoolbag, Mandy." Mandy relaxed her grip and dropped the bag on the desk.

"Stay, Mandy." She felt the dog crawl under her wheelchair as she often did at home, as if recess had been called. It was the place she liked best, away from the world, from which she could peer under and about, her long body hanging out from all sides, yet feeling completely hidden from anyone around her.

Feeling a surge of confidence because of the partner lying flat under her chair, Samantha had known from the beginning it would be this way. Through the rigorous training, through the commands of heel, sit, fetch, come, stay, Mandy's almost bored expression had been a declaration of acceptance, as if she were sitting through a class she had attended before. Yet, when she looked at Sam through those soulful brown eyes that were now closed in a half doze, it was as if she were saying, "Go ahead, if it makes you feel better, thinking you've trained me."

The three short weeks of training, of carrying crutches from one end of the room to the other, of picking up everything from tissues to pencils, had led them here.

"Hi, girl," a classmate greeted Mandy.

"What's her name?" another asked.

Mandy's large tail thumped from under the wheelchair as heads bent down, and eyes peered under, and hands gently patted whatever part of the dog still remained to be touched.

Samantha smiled her hellos. Mandy always seemed to know what to do with introductions and good-byes. She would frolic around with excited greetings, quick licks to the face and hands, and then the good-bye was usually forlorn, ears down, close to the head, tail at half-mast.

Mr. Luber stood before the blackboard, elaborately writing out his name. He covered the black slate, as if it were a moving canopy.

"Good girl, Mandy," Sam whispered, letting her fingers trail down under the wheelchair. "You'll like school. They might even give you a degree."

She pictured Mandy walking up to the stage in the auditorium, a red graduation cap on her head, her long sleek coat freshly brushed and washed, brilliant with autumn hues, the cap slipping back over the long ears. A smile edged its way across Sam's face and moved over the high cheekbones. Her eyes, sometimes light, like faint touches of spring, sometimes dark with storm clouds, seemed uncertain now. She looked about for a familiar face. There was none.

She took out her notebook and wrote down the schedule of classes for the day.

"I wish I could be with you today," her father had said before he left for work. "I wanted to take the day off."

She knew he couldn't. Her mother had driven her to school in the station wagon, with Mandy panting all the way to Scot High, through the partly opened back window.

"Are you sure Mandy will be O.K. in school?" her mother had asked. Sam could still see her worried face looking out the window. What she was really asking was, "Will *you* be all right, Sam? Will any of us be all right again?"

Those who made the rules at Scot High had said yes, it would be O.K. for Mandy to attend classes with Samantha. She kept repeating that to herself, over and over as the morning drew to a close. Yes, it would be O.K. for both of them.

As she moved from class to class, she found herself tensing with Mandy as each new bell opened and closed the classroom session. The bells and loudspeaker system bounced off the walls in the corridor and seemed to grow in intensity. Mandy would look around nervously, as if she were back out in the woods again, the guns popping off. Over and over again, Sam stilled her nervousness with her soothing hands. She could feel Mandy's breath growing quicker, the panting heavier, the eyes large with excitement.

"It's O.K., Mandy, we're together. I won't leave you. There are no guns." Over and over, and then the dog would answer with an eager tongue-licking and they would again begin their journey down the halls.

Samantha had never felt this sense of control before. She had never felt the power to change what went on around her, though at the moment she didn't know what she would want changed except to walk. Yes, that might be the only change. With Mandy, she felt a sense of command, a sense of having to know what she wanted so that she could convey it to the dog. Yet, she was smart enough to realize that Mandy allowed her this power. And if she chose to, Mandy could take it away as quickly as she had given it.

Sam kept her eyes on the clock toward 11:30. The morning had suddenly turned slow. She felt tired, a fatigue she wasn't used to. She had pushed past her usual resource of strength. The excitement, the constant pace, had drained her. There seemed little time to get from one class to another. Her classes were spaced from one end of the building to the extreme other end. The distance spread over several blocks. It was a race between classes that Mandy enjoyed more than Sam. For Sam, it seemed a trip through a maze of pushing, scrambling bodies. They were up there. She was down here. They moved about knowingly. Her wheelchair didn't seem to know its way.

It was right before lunch that she thought about the toilet. She had managed to push it out of her mind as part of the training process she had set up for herself. She couldn't get in the toilet by herself. The doorway wasn't wide enough for her wheelchair. She had discovered that during her preschool interview. Her parents had wanted to say something about it. Samantha chose not to. The last thing she wanted to be was a problem. Problems were noticed. It was her desire to be as inconspicuous as possible, to blend in with the others, to bring as little attention to herself as was necessary. She was confident that Mandy would soon become a permanent fixture and gradually disappear from the limelight. Then she could go as she had always gone . . . unnoticed.

Her mother had devised a plan to outwit the toilets. Plan A involved Sam's calling her mother. Her mother would pick her up and take her home. This Plan A would keep her mother housebound all day. The alternate Plan B was for Sam to become friendly with a couple of her classmates who could help her out of the chair and into the girls' room. Plan B held its risks. Sam could be dropped. She knew several disabled who had been dropped by well-meaning helpers who weren't quite sure what they were doing. Serious injury to the skin and bones was the result for some. She didn't want that.

Samantha had devised Plan C which she shared with her mother, who looked upon it with some doubt. Sam had learned a lot more about mental control during her months of rehabilitation. There were paraplegics around her who had trained themselves to go for long periods of time without using toilet facilities when there were none that were accessible to them. She had decided to try to do the same thing, to control her bodily functions until she returned home each day. This meant not thinking about it. She was thinking about it now. Plan C would never work if she kept this up.

Ms. Jenkins, the English teacher, looked her way every now and then. While everyone was taking down the next day's assignments, she came over to Sam and kneeled down beside the wheelchair. She stroked Mandy as she spoke.

"Is there anything you need, Sam?" she asked.

Sam thought of the toilet. She needed to use it desperately, yet asking this teacher seemed the last thing she could do. The words got stuck in her throat. She shook her head no and smiled politely.

"Please ask me if there is."

Sam was tempted. Sue Jenkins's green eyes were so honest, so direct, as they looked into her own. But then Samantha looked over to the girl sitting next to her. She was watching them. It seemed the entire class had grown suddenly silent and turned their attention toward Samantha and Ms. Jenkins.

"I'm just fine," she said again, anxious to convince Ms. Jenkins and end the conversation. The English teacher seemed satisfied and returned to her desk.

The clock weaved its way toward 12:00. She ate her lunch at a table crowded with faces she had never seen before. She ate her sandwich but carefully avoided a beverage. She felt less comfortable than she had in the morning. The girls drifted off to the girls' room. There's no problem, no problem at all, Sam tried to convince herself. Her bladder began to make itself known, protesting Plan C. Samantha took Mandy to the back of the school after lunch. The dog relieved herself under a large maple tree. "At least one of us has accommodations," she joked, taking the dog in her long arms, but a sense of panic was splitting the day.

It was while going to her next class that Samantha saw a small crowd gathered around the boys' toilet. She and Mandy tried to work their way around the group pressed closely together, but somehow the bodies parted and pulled Sam in. Mandy followed begrudgingly. Uncomfortable and excited by the moving crowd, the dog then tried to find a small patch of light by pushing forward. Sam followed her, trying to pull Mandy back. Elbows whizzed past Sam's head.

"Mandy, come back here," she called, trying to regain control of the dog who seemed determined to dig her way out of the tunnel of pushing bodies. Mandy finally stopped when she reached the large opening in front of the crowd. "Excuse me, excuse me," Sam whispered, seeing only legs and jackets and few faces as she followed Mandy's reddish tail to the front.

Samantha saw the sign first. She saw it because it was impossible not to see, with its big blue lettering and large white background. At least the sign that read, **No one in a wheelchair can get in these toilets,** had blue lettering. The other signs propped up against the wall were printed in bold black and flashy red.

The giggles from around Sam fell like waves about her shoulders. She felt her face grow hot and she touched Mandy's head for support. "Come on, girl, let's get out of here."

But Mandy wouldn't move. It was almost as if she were reading the signs herself, her eyes wide and concentrating, staring at the boards ahead which seemed to be everywhere. One of the signs was being held by a boy with bright red hair and a splattering of freckles across his face. He was sitting in a wheelchair. She might have liked the look of him had not the sign been held in his lap.

He had the build of an athlete, or maybe someone who lifted weights. He was slim, with his legs looking almost too long for the wheelchair he sat in, yet his arms and chest were well developed.

His eyes were an angry brown, and he held the sign in front of him, propped on his lap like a large tablecloth. He wheeled back and forth, pacing the floor in front of the boys' toilet, doing it so quickly and so often, it seemed that there were two of him. Another sign read, **Make this toilet accessible.** It was leaning up against the water fountain.

If Samantha could have run from the spot, she would have. In one of her stories she might have created a moment of magic where everyone would have disappeared, the boy with the insistent eyes, the signs, the crowd, pointing, laughing, murmuring in confusion, cheering, a mixture of emotions running through it. She would have, with her wand of words, made them disappear. And had the comfort of disappearing herself.

But she couldn't go anywhere. The crowd around her had her wedged tightly, and all she could do was sit helplessly watching the boy with the long arms hold the sign higher and higher so that everyone could see.

For an endless moment all she could think of was that now they knew, all of them around her. They knew, as certainly as she knew it, that she was unable to use the girls' room. And because they knew, they would look her way.

She had never wanted that, and she didn't want it now. Samantha finally managed to turn her chair around and was about to leave when she froze to the sound of an arrogant voice behind her.

"Hey, you, you in the wheelchair. Don't leave. Come on up here and help me out."

Sam looked back over her shoulder, feeling the pressure of the sudden silence around her. Mandy stopped as if by command and also looked toward the demanding voice.

"Come on. Two of us is better than one. Take that sign over there." He pointed to **Make this toilet accessible,** which seemed to be quite content leaning against the water fountain. He seemed to assume she would join him.

Still Sam didn't move. Her eyes were now half-closed, the blueness in them like ominous slits. Shut up . . . shut **up** . . . the words ran silently through her mind, fighting to escape.

"Come on," he challenged her. He sensed her fear. He was holding it in front of her.

Some of the crowd urged her on. But Samantha, head bent down, wheeled her way out of the crowd, tasting hate for the first time.

How dare he link the two of them together? She felt the tears sting at her eyes as she called to Mandy. He in his wheelchair had joined her to him with some invisible chain. She didn't even know his name, had never even seen him before. Yet everyone witnessing his protest was lumping them together in one package.

He with his signs had brought all eyes to his wheelchair and to the problems of his wheelchair. And now to hers, too. And none of them would ever forget that she, too, couldn't use the toilet. They would always keep that image in their mind, whenever they saw her. He had pointed a finger at himself, but he had also pointed it at her.

Samantha wheeled into the front office. "May I make a telephone call?" she asked the woman at the front desk. She tried to still the trembling in her voice, the spasms in her legs. Mandy hung about her like a worried mother, now and then sniffing at her hair, raising herself on the arms of Sam's chair, leaning over to look full into her face.

Sam took the phone and dialed her home. "Mother," she said, "please come and get me. I don't feel well." When she hung up, she looked back toward the hall. The crowd had thinned. She could see him clearly now, sitting like a king in front of his subjects, his red hair picking up flashes of light from the hall lights above him. She hated him for sitting there exposing his needs in front of everyone. She hated him even more for exposing hers.

4 ———

She swept her hair up in back of her head.
Beads of perspiration danced across her forehead.

"You'll have to excuse me. I just came from
Heartbreak Hill. I had intended to be back here
earlier." The long, slim fingers reached out
toward Mandy and stroked her ears.

Samantha followed the graceful figure into the
small apartment. She smiled as Sue Jenkins kept
tucking a piece of blond hair back behind one ear.

"It's really O.K." Samantha tried to make her
comfortable. "I'm a little early." She wanted the
interview to go well. It was her first assignment
since joining the school paper. She had come up
with the idea of doing a feature on Ms. Jenkins after a brief discussion between the two of them on
marathon running.

"You run?" Samantha had asked of the English

teacher with the pert nose that housed a couple of neat brown freckles. She liked her laugh. It reminded her of a succession of high notes, the high white notes on a piano. Sam had liked Ms. Jenkins from the moment she had come into her English class.

She had never again asked Sam if she needed help, but managed each time she was in her English class to have a few moments where they might speak together. Ms. Jenkins was easy to talk to . . . and Sam found herself holding back less and less. Sometimes she felt she was being dishonest with the teacher, for she had led her to believe that everything was going along fine when actually the problem of the bathrooms still loomed in the shadows each day she was in school.

Once, as they often did in the moments between classes, during a reaching-out, getting-to-know-you kind of conversation, Samantha had confided her love for writing. The loneliness, the isolation, but also the challenge.

"Just like running along," Ms. Jenkins had answered. That's how Sam had first learned of Sue Jenkins's love for marathon running. Somewhere during the laughter they shared, the germ of an idea had begun to grow in Samantha's mind. She sensed a devotion, almost a fanatic commitment on Sue Jenkins's part to running. She felt there was a story there. The school newspaper editor had said, "Go to it."

"Watch out for the rugs," Ms. Jenkins cautioned. Samantha steered around the scattered throw rugs in the small living room. A macrame wall piece hung from the ceiling on one side of the wall. It looked as if it were still being worked on. Some healthy green plants sat showing off on a shelf under a large window overlooking a busy street. A couch, which looked as if it could be pulled out into a bed, occupied the middle of the living room. Large, brightly covered throw pillows lay haphazardly around the room, some on chairs, some on the floor, as if they were expecting visitors to sit upon them.

"I'll be right back. I feel I could drink a river." Ms. Jenkins's trim body disappeared through the doorway and Sam heard ice cubes clinking. Sue Jenkins didn't know it, but she was partly responsible for Sam's returning to school and being able to put up with Johnny Jay, who seemed to be everywhere with his signs . . . in front of the toilets which had not been altered, down in the driveway after school trying to get petitions signed. Wherever she went, his freckles were before her. He always smiled her way. She worked hard at not smiling back.

She had returned to school the next day, after the first introduction to Johnny and his crusade, reluctant, but realizing she couldn't stay away forever. She held the dim hope that perhaps he would get tired and just go away. Now and then in passing him, she felt a grim satisfaction in separating herself from his purposes, as if she were saying to the entire world around her, "We're different. We're not the same."

He was getting nowhere anyway, with his Don Quixote battle. Let him fight for his toilets. She had found her own way. She had mastered a certain amount of self-control that enabled her to go through the entire day without having to depend on anyone.

But it was Ms. Jenkins who had put Johnny Jay and his activities into the shadows. One day, holding Sam's composition, she had suggested that Sam write for the school newspaper. She had done more than suggest. Sue Jenkins had taken both the wheelchair and Samantha in tow, pushing and talking excitedly about Sam's talent, pulling up the window shades on it. Then they were in the art room that was also used for the school paper's editorial meetings.

Samantha thought about the forcefulness of the teacher as she actually shoved her into the limelight at the meeting. Her determination might ordinarily have annoyed Sam, especially when it came to something as private as her writing. But the high, generous laughter of Ms. Jenkins behind her stilled any antagonism she might have felt. The teacher's sudden joy often reminded her how seldom people laughed.

"Oh, I am sorry to keep you waiting." Tiny fingers pressed a glass of cool lemonade into Sam's hands. "I was so excited when you called, to think you wanted to interview me. You know, in the fifteen years I've taught here, no one has ever done this." The face opposite Sam's was flushed, the green eyes held a sparkle that reminded her of a child's at a birthday party. She moved so quickly, with the grace of a dancer, putting the napkin there, the tray here, petting Mandy who was now rolling over playfully on her back. She seemed to fill the apartment with bits of herself, as if there were a crowd of people in it, when actually Ms. Jenkins lived there alone.

Sam watched Mandy doing the warming up for both of them, rubbing her head against the hand that stroked her, pressing against Sue Jenkins so fully that she nearly pushed the small body off balance.

Samantha took out her pad and pencil from her shoulder bag, the little edges of her nerves relaxing, and putting the big bag down on her lap, used it as a table to write on.

"I think everyone in the school," she began, "would like to know something about your marathon running and why you run."

Mandy had settled at the edge of Ms. Jenkins's small feet, but her nose and closed eyes were facing Sam's, the ears now and then perking to show she was on alert.

"Why I run?" Ms. Jenkins ran the words over, her eyes closing slightly, but with a faraway look as if the answer were out there, beyond the walls of the living room.

Samantha gave her time. She had gone to the newspaper meetings, sat through the layout and planning, learned how to set the headlines and how to conduct the interview, just so that one day, like today, she could be sitting across from someone interesting, ready to open his or her life up to her readers.

She pictured her by-line, "Samantha Lee Anderson," all the while wishing it were a more glamorous or less common name. Once she had counted the Andersons in the telephone directory and stopped at two hundred.

Ms. Jenkins sat with her hands clasped behind her head, her eyes gazing at the ceiling as if she were examining the universe. "So much to tell, and so little," she shrugged. "I guess at first I ran to keep in shape. You know, at my age, it gets quite easy to develop a roll around the middle." She leaned forward toward Sam. "I always took advantage of the summers to get out and exercise, tennis and swimming, but in the winter, well, it seemed I was just getting lazy about ME!" Her voice exploded as she pointed to herself.

"I do a lot of sitting at that desk in English class and my feet would get edgy, as if they wanted to go off dashing somewhere. I ran one day and it felt terrific. I felt terrific." The green eyes lit up with satisfaction as if she had just answered a test question correctly.

"How do you feel when you run?"

"Refreshed. Beautifully refreshed. As if I've just taken a cool shower."

Samantha was surprised. Sometimes after writing a good article or story, she felt the same way . . . refreshed. She knew better than to break her teacher's train of thought with her own personal observation. "How much do you run a day?"

"Oh." Sue put her hands around her knees. Sam noted how seriously she took each question. "I started with about two miles a day, then I went to about four or five miles. I guess I run about five miles a day. Once I get into a schedule, I run over twenty miles a week. That's when I'm training for a marathon run."

"Why do you do it?" Samantha knew, as a good reporter, that sometimes she had to go deeper than the top answer given her. Ms. Jenkins's first answer as to why didn't really go deep enough. There had to be more of a reason to endure such rigorous training, especially for the longer marathons. She felt it unfair probing perhaps deeper than Ms. Jenkins wanted to go. She pushed her guilt aside. Her readers would want to know.

"Well . . ." Ms. Jenkins's silver-blond hair disappeared around the corner again. She returned with a plate full of cookies. She sat down on the floor next to Mandy, looking more like a little girl than a teacher in her mid-thirties. A thin line of excitement flashed over her face. "Samantha, I run to be alone. And when I'm alone, I'm working toward all kinds of exciting things to broaden me." She poined to herself. "I think while I run. I dream while I run. You know what I mean? It's lovely, and yet lonely. Sometimes painful. Sometimes boring. But it's mine, entirely to do with what I please. I can be as good as I want to be, or as bad. It depends on how much I want to put into training, into the commitment of it. I guess it's just that. It's a commitment." She laughed, running up the scale again. "Does that make sense?"

"It does make sense to me." Sam used a tone that was more friend to friend than teacher to student. "How do you feel when you run in a marathon?" Sam continued.

"Sometimes numb, sometimes my feet and lungs feel almost as if they're burning up. But then, oh, there are times when it's like flying above myself, as if I were on a cloud looking down at me, and there I am running my head off, loving the competitiveness of it all, when sometimes I'm the only one I'm competing against."

Sam suddenly wished she could have that feeling. Writing brought her an exhilaration, and it was lonely, just as Ms. Jenkins sometimes found running. But the challenge of competing in a marathon run . . . in pushing oneself past the point of endurance. She realized sitting there across from Sue Jenkins that she had never done that in her life, never pushed herself past the point of anything.

"And what if the other runners in the marathon are better than you are."

"Then next time I'll just train my head off so that I can be better than they are. It's really just my two legs on my body and my training and everything I've done that will make the difference against the other runners."

Sam remembered the advice of a veteran reporter on the school paper who had warned her not to stay too long. She glanced at her watch, then decided there was time for one more question.

"When will you be running another marathon?"

"I'll be entering the spring marathon coming up right here through town." She leaned forward as if she were sharing an important moment. "It will be held in April, and it's going to go past Heartbreak Hill, right over the three miles of the steepest, toughest hill in town. We runners call it Heartbreak Hill because it's so close to the end of the marathon and so very difficult to get past. If any one of us is going to drop out, we know it will be while trying to climb that hill." She paused and her voice grew soft. "Heartbreak Hill will be the turning point. I feel if I can make it over that hill, I can do anything."

Samantha just sat there spellbound. For a moment, she forgot that it was she who opened the interview and must end it. Finally, she closed her notebook and put her notes away in her pocketbook.

"Ms. Jenkins, I want to thank you for all this time." She went toward the door. As if the moving wheels had issued a silent command, Mandy stood by the door, holding it open with her body.

Sue Jenkins followed Sam out into the street. "Can I give you a lift home?" she offered.

Sam started down the street, with Mandy jumping through the leaves which crunched beneath her feet. "Thanks, but I'm not far from home. I'd enjoy walking."

She saw the startled look on Ms. Jenkins's face.

Her teacher had shared so much of herself today, Sam felt like sharing back. "I just use the language of the world," she said lightly, knowing the word *walk* had seemed like the most unlikely thing she would do. Then she waved and continued down the street.

Sam and Mandy were a noisy twosome. The leaves were parched. A November chill left the fallen bits of branches thirsty and burned, as toast left in the toaster a moment too long. The wind was neatly gathering them together, sweeping them off to the side of the road, instinctively getting ready for the winter snows. The sky took on a dark mood, and though it was getting dusky earlier now, Sam knew these were clouds holding rain. She wondered if her sense of independence was worth the soaking she was going to get.

A car's insistent honking brought Sam's attention toward the street. Mandy jumped around excitedly at the noise, then, like a mother hen protecting its young, put her body in front of Sam's as the car pulled over to the curb.

Samantha saw Johnny's red hair and then the freckled face beaming on the passenger's side of the car. He was alone.

"Want a lift?"

It was about that time the first drop of rain chose to fall. It splashed loudly down on the wheelchair as if to get Samantha's immediate attention. And then one drop folded into another. Mandy stood still, guarding Sam, and watched Johnny Jay with curious eyes.

"What about it?" Johnny reached over and opened the car door.

Samantha hadn't counted on the rain. She watched the remaining leaves slip from the trees and fall on the street in front of her, wet and slippery. Her first instinct was that she would rather drown than enter his car. But then the rain grew heavier, almost as if Johnny were controlling it, as he tried to control everything else around him. She still had several wet, slippery streets to go.

Mandy growled as Johnny bent out of the car and pulled Sam's wheelchair toward him. "Tell Mandy to stay. Let's get you and the wheelchair settled in."

Sam ordered Mandy back.

Johnny slid back toward the driver's seat. Sam transferred over to the passenger side of the car. She had never driven before with a driver who also used a wheelchair. She looked at him, hoping he had bit off more than he could chew. Mandy and her wheelchair still remained on the wet curb.

"Can you fold the wheelchair up from where you are?"

Sam nodded and folded the chair beside the car. Johnny drew closer to her again, his strong arms all about her as he bent forward, pushing her seat forward, and slid the chair behind them into the back seat. She noticed then that there was no back seat in the car, but instead a large, wide space that was now filled with two chairs.

Mandy stood there, forlorn, on the outside, not

liking the entire matter at all. Sam called to her, and the front seat was filled with her long body. She was half in Sam's lap, her head and tongue pointed slightly over Johnny's head.

"Sort of crowded," he laughed.

At last they agreed on something.

"Where do you live?" he asked.

"On Burchard Avenue," she answered.

"Did someone drive you here? That's quite a distance."

"No," she said proudly. "I came here to interview Ms. Jenkins for the school paper by myself."

She felt proud knowing that. She wanted him to know it, too. If she had dared to be honest with him, she would have added, "At least I'm not wasting time fighting windmills." She decided not to say it.

Mandy now crouched between the two of them, trying to make herself very small. Her wet ears first turned toward Sam, then to Johnny, as she followed their conversation like an attentive listener.

"Where are your signs?" she asked sarcastically. The words slipped out.

"In the back," he answered. "How'd you get to be in a wheelchair?"

The question shocked her. No one had asked her that since she had become disabled. It was as if he had a key to a door never opened before. She felt it twist inside her.

"Diving." Her voice was a whisper, as the key unlocked the door to the past.

That day at the lake, it seemed so very long ago, when the others had tried to catch up with her long legs and quick pace as she ran past the small boats anchored at the dock. She could still hear their laughter, the laughter of new friends found at the summer resort she and her brother Bucky and her parents had come to for the week. The old shyness that had haunted her through childhood slipped away softly on that bright summer day as she dared to be whoever she chose to be.

She recalled so clearly, even now, every detail, the feeling of urgency that she must be the first to touch the magic of the blue lake and dip into its coolness. The excitement of being accepted easily in a strange place with new faces still clung to her as she sped into the sunlight. Even as she dived off the side of the dock, she knew. She had never looked back or around or even too keenly in front. Her eyes, partly closed, shielding her from the early-morning sunlight, saw little more than a shimmering lake.

There had been nothing else to see—no sign to warn her, Shallow End. Not an arrow pointing to Danger—Waterline Low. It was as if it were a big secret between the lake and the sun cutting into it.

Samantha had discovered the lake's secret as a terrifying blackness closed over her. The laughter that had once ridden behind her was replaced by the silence of disaster. She would always remember her mother's terrified scream, "Sam," the soft lake water covering her mouth, her arms, her chest, but nothing, no sense of anything from the waist down. It had been like that ever since.

"It must have been tough for you." Johnny's voice was gentle as if he had read her thoughts. His eyes had lost their anger.

The drive was short, but it felt long. He had a way of stretching time, using it. Even when he was quiet, she felt he was directing the situation.

She pointed to the house with the large fence around it. Johnny pulled the car up into the driveway. Mandy didn't like the cramped quarters. As soon as Sam opened the door, Mandy jumped past her and out onto the lawn.

"How the heck do you go to the toilet?" Johnny asked abruptly as he helped pull her chair out from the back seat, sliding it down on the ground beside her. His arms were long and strong, and as he leaned over, she felt the closeness of him. "You must have the same trouble as I do, getting into the toilets. It's impossible. You can't get through the doorways."

She cringed with each accusation, biting her lip, determined not to give him the satisfaction of an answer. Why wouldn't his eyes let go of her?

He was waiting for her answer. She struggled to open her wheelchair, bending toward the curb, wanting just to slip into her chair and get out of there.

Sam felt his hand touch her arm. It was light, gentle, compared to the dark searching eyes that she was running from. She wrenched her arm away and slipped into her open chair.

"Why don't you help me? Two of us might stand a better chance!"

All Sam wanted to do was get into the house before he said another word.

"You didn't answer my question." He was leaning out the window.

Now anger rose in her. Free from the closeness of him, she could give him an answer. "Don't you ever stop being disabled?" She replaced his question with one of her own. "Are you disabled twenty-four hours a day?"

For a change, the shock was on his face.

"Mandy," she called and turned her back on the car, "take my bag." But Mandy surprised her by taking off up the driveway and scratching at the front door.

She heard Johnny's parting words long after he left. She knew he wouldn't let her have the last word. "Whether you like it or not, Samantha, you're one of us. If I don't get into that toilet, neither do you, not unless you drag yourself across the floor." The visual image of that hurt her more than his words.

Her father was waiting for her at the door. "Wasn't that Johnny Jay," he asked, "the boy who's causing all the trouble at Scot High School?"

"Yes, he gave me a ride home from the interview. It was raining." She felt she needed to offer an excuse.

Her father's face tightened and a tiny line of fear circled his mouth. "You know," he said quietly, but it was the kind of quiet that held a power behind it, "I can't afford any trouble with the school. My contract comes up in the spring." And then, as if he wanted to repeat the words once again so that they should be understood, he added, "Don't get involved with the kid, Sam. He'll only bring you trouble. Maybe trouble to all of us."

Sam wheeled into her bedroom and closed the door behind her. "Get my slippers, Mandy," she called.

Mandy didn't move. Instead she squatted near Sam's desk, wearing a very stuffed expression. Her mouth, though closed, seemed swollen. She sat with tail wagging, but still not obeying.

Sam wheeled over to her. She bent down. Something stuck out of Mandy's mouth. She put out her hand, palm up. "Drop it, Mandy," she ordered.

A wallet tumbled from Mandy's lips and dropped into Sam's hand. Samantha opened the wallet. In the first plastic holder was a picture of a little boy. He had red hair and brown eyes. He looked familiar. In the second plastic holder was the picture of a boy she knew quite well. He was sitting in a wheelchair holding a sign. He was surrounded by other sign-holders.

Johnny Jay. "Mandy. Bad. You took Johnny's wallet," she scolded the dog whose ears now tucked themselves in. Sam waved her finger crossly at Mandy, but a mischievous smile crept about her lips. She could see him, he with his so sure expression, searching through the car.

"Let him look." Sam put the wallet in her schoolbag. "He'll just have to wait until tomorrow." Her hand touched the notebook with Sue Jenkins's interview in it. Sam took the book out and began to review her notes.

She took the cover off her typewriter and typed the words "Heartbreak Hill" at the top of the page. She sat there typing until dusk filled the room with evening shadows.

5 ─────

She stood there on the road waiting for Samantha's wheelchair to come into view. It had become a familiar beacon to her during these long January weeks.

Sue Jenkins straightened her bright red sweat suit and tucked the warm winter hat around her ears. Only her silver-blond hair showed in the back, trailing down the jacket like an exclamation point.

Samantha had called only a couple of days after the interview. At first Sue thought Sam wanted some additional information regarding the newspaper story. She was eager to see what Samantha would create from what she had told her. The young student's style in writing had a certain wistfulness, a flair that set it apart from many of the other students.

But it wasn't because of the interview that Samantha had contacted her. She had surprised her by asking to work out in the mornings, to wheel while Sue ran.

She knew better than to ask her why. Samantha had a hundred little doors in front her which she clicked open and shut at will. Step too close . . . they shut without warning.

All this time, Sue had watched Sam's wheelchair zigzagging through the tight aisles of the classrooms with Mandy close behind. The chair was always there, reminding Sue how inadequate the school was to its needs. And then there was Johnny Jay, never letting any of them forget.

Yet it was Samantha she wanted to know better, Samantha with her gentle manner, with the big eyes that often took on a sadness that was difficult to meet. Sue tried to picture Samantha standing. She seemed tall, even sitting in the wheelchair. She wondered just how tall she was. She felt guilty wondering. She tried not to dwell on such thoughts, but they darted in front of her without warning.

She often found herself staring at Sam, watching the long, graceful hands guide the wheelchair, watching the willowy figure dart in between her rushing classmates. As if by some magic, one who seemed so fragile survived the change of classes and continued to remain in one piece day after day.

Sam's face always had a glow to it, as if she had just come out of the sun. Had she been standing, she would have been the type of girl you had to turn around and look at twice. Sue Jenkins knew that the wheelchair changed all that, yet she didn't understand why. At gym, she'd see Samantha on the side, watching. She'd picture her leaping toward a basket. Mental images that she stubbornly cast aside kept popping back into view. Sam dancing. Sam running.

During the past couple of months, they had begun to know each other better. Three mornings a week they met, in the early-dawn hours, getting up while the sky was still smoky black and small lights touched the homes of early-morning risers. They would push past the cold and the darkness, and while Samantha wheeled and Sue ran, they began to chat, and trade bits of each other's lives.

On Saturdays they met in the afternoon for about an hour. But during it all, Samantha never told her why. Sue read an urgency in her eyes, as if there were an important message there to be decoded only by the right trusted person. She wanted to be that person. She wanted Samantha's friendship.

Sue sat down on the curb and tucked her heavy socks underneath her trousers. She had been reading up on wheelchairs. She knew nothing about them when she had first met Sam. She didn't even know how much they cost. That was the first bit of information she had acquired. She was amazed to find a wheelchair could cost anywhere from $100 to $2000 and over. The cheaper ones were not to be depended on for too long, the more expensive were the electric that moved about quickly through motor control. Somewhere in between had been Samantha's wheelchair, about $500, which was no little amount of money considering the repairs and the fact that it would probably have to be replaced as the years went on.

She began to subscribe to some magazines and newspapers concerning the disabled, magazines that Johnny Jay had told her about. Headlines of events she didn't even know took place splashed across the pages. She wondered why she hadn't known what was going on before. Where was the news in her own local newspapers? Until Samantha and Johnny had become part of the school, Sue and the other teachers had known practically nothing about how to handle disabled students. In a way she resented it. She thought she had received an education for becoming a teacher, and yet here she was, ignorant of the needs of some of her pupils. She wondered how many other teachers suffered the same confusion.

Sitting there, she felt so ignorant, as if she should start all over again. There were new laws now, laws that had not been in existence when she began teaching. Years ago, no one had even thought of architectural barriers in schools. No one ever had to adjust to disabled students in public schools. They just weren't there.

Sue picked at her memory, trying to remember just one child in a wheelchair whom she had taught before Sam. She couldn't remember any.

Where were the blind students, the deaf ones,

the ones in wheelchairs? Special schools? Home? Not learning anything at all?

Sue rubbed her gloved hands together. Now the law said it must change. Now there must be readers for the blind and interpreters for the deaf. *Now* meant the disabled coming into public schools to learn, and she, as a teacher, felt helpless, not knowing what it was she was expected to do.

Each day she faced Samantha in class, she asked herself again and again, What can I do to make it easier? and yet when she went to Samantha for answers, she was faced with a closed door. Sam talked about everything with her but her disability. And that was the one thing she needed to talk about . . . both of them needed to do that.

Only last week at an in-service meeting did the principal share his problems with the teachers. It was Johnny Jay and his signs that had brought it all to a head. "I don't know where to go for money." The principal shook his head. "Opening up those toilets and making them accessible seems impossible under our school budget now. If we don't comply, we might lose any government funding we have acquired."

The questions around the table at that meeting seemed unending and continued to haunt her. How do you make a building entirely accessible? No one seemed to know the answer. What about steps, and ramps and elevators? What kind of door works best for someone in a wheelchair? What books do you read to find the right answers? What do you do when a solution that works for one disability causes problems for another disability?

Even going over them a week later brought few solutions. Sue sat there feeling more inadequate as the questions nagged at her. How do you present information so that blind and deaf people can determine where they are? What about fire alarms and emergency warnings? She shuddered to think of the deaf when the bell rang . . . of the blind when the red emergency light blinked. But the question that was asked over and over remained unanswered even now—how to know what to do first with the limited funds at hand. Where to spend the money . . . which was the most important problem?

And then there was Johnny Jay every day reminding them. Sue felt the squeeze along with everyone else. Amidst the confusion, the teachers threw up their hands in dismay, not knowing exactly where they fit in. Sue and so many teachers around her felt the urgent need to turn it around, to help bring about the change, but they didn't know how to take the first step.

Running with Sam had taught her something about pushing a chair. It had put her on a much more intimate basis as the daily workouts left them both breathless and drained. She had shared Sam's heavy breathing as their sessions grew longer, the pain on her face. Who could expect people to use their arms to propel their entire body plus the weight of all that metal? It was a silent story that was told to her as they pushed past five miles, then six a day, the inert object of the wheelchair, Sam's arms like the wings of a plane, yet not flying, but pushing, and gradually doing it easier and easier until lately, Sue felt the wheelchair keeping up with her without any problem at all.

Sometimes Sam would question her about diet. At those times, Sue felt perhaps she was doing an in-depth article, a bigger feature on marathon running, one in which she had to become involved. But then the intensity in the blue eyes, the determination around the set mouth, gave hint of a much larger mission.

Sue was growing uneasy. As the months drew on, she felt her student was expecting something of her, something she didn't know about yet. She didn't want to let her down. She almost wished she could turn to Sam and say, "Come on, Sam, why are you doing this? Tell me, so we can help each other. What do you want me to help you with?" But having Sam slam a door in her face frightened her more than not knowing.

Sam's wheelchair turned the corner of Yellowstone Road, a small, silvery square with a bright blue sweat suit filling the inside.

There was one thing Sue had made up her mind to set straight today. And if Sam shut the door, she'd just knock it right open again. The matter of the toilet.

She ran toward her, and without a word they set off down the quiet, tree-lined streets, past the apartment houses, the shopping plaza, and parking spaces, zigzagging through the sleeping town.

Sue ran in the street to keep Mandy and Sam company.

"How long is that April marathon?" Sam asked in between pushes on the chair, her long arms reaching with long, strong strokes.

"Twenty-six miles."

Sue looked over at Sam. And then she knew, as if the answer had been there all along, standing there bright and fresh, almost laughing at her, it was so obvious.

"Didn't we do eight miles Saturday?" Sam asked.

"Over that."

"How long does it take to run the marathon?" Sam wasn't letting it go.

"Depends. It's over a three-hour course."

Silence, except for the sound of the wheels against the street and Mandy's excited panting.

Sue wanted to squeeze the words out of her. You want to run it, don't you, Sam? You want to run Heartbreak Hill? She kept a little ahead, for if she stayed at Sam's side, she would see it in her eyes . . . Sam would see she knew.

"Is Heartbreak Hill far from here?"

Sue's heart quickened. "No," she said nonchalantly. "In the marathon it stretches toward the eighteenth mile, but from here," she stopped and looked back toward the country club golf course, "it's about three miles that way." She pointed with her gloved hand.

As if by mutual understanding they both turned toward the golf course, as if there were no other way to go. Sue looked over at Samantha. Her cheeks were red, her eyes had an unusual fire to them. Her dark hair had almost a wild look, spilling out from under her hat with the blue pom-pom at the top.

A thread of uneasiness began to wind in and out of Sue's mind when she thought about Sam possibly participating in the marathon. In all the marathons she had competed in, she never remembered seeing anyone at the starting line or finishing line in a wheelchair. She wondered if it would present a problem. Then quickly, she abandoned the thought, angry with herself that she had become so questioning lately. If Sam wanted to compete, there just wouldn't be a problem. There couldn't be.

"Do you think I have endurance now?" Sam asked. "After all this training, do you think I can keep it going like this far past the eight miles we've done so far?"

"I think you have as much endurance as anyone I know."

"Including you."

"You bet."

Again silence. The thin line between them was now growing thinner, like a sliver of ice lining a twig, growing weaker and melting under an afternoon sun. Each now became lost in her own thoughts. Sue savored these moments to think, to explore, to wonder, almost to feel herself growing.

Samantha, too, seemed far away. Sue suddenly realized she didn't hear Mandy's footsteps behind her. Samantha sensed it at the same time. They both turned around, for the moment, bewildered. Had she been in front or in back? It had been but seconds ago that Sam had seen the wild ears flapping.

The sound of a desperate horn, then the piercing screech of brakes, combined with a series of frantic barks, set them both heading toward the corner. Sue saw Sam's face go white. The street suddenly seemed strangely quiet, as though the frightening sounds heard only moments before had been but their imagination.

"Oh, no, oh, no," Sam kept crying over and over as they turned the corner, both barely daring to look toward the car which sat in the middle of the street, its engine still running.

"Is she your dog? She's O.K. Honest, lady, she's O.K. I hit the horn and it seemed to confuse her. First she was there, near the car, then she was in front of it. I never saw a dog move so fast."

Mandy was sitting in the middle of the street, panting as if she had just run in a marathon herself. The man was kneeling beside her, stroking her ears. The car sat silent, waiting, quite innocent looking considering what horrors it had nearly beset upon poor Mandy.

Sam was there first, with Mandy suddenly coming to life, bouncing on her lap, licking her face, brushing away the tears that were flowing from both Sam and Sue.

"I didn't hit her. It was close. I was just turning the corner. I think if I hadn't hit the horn, everything would have been O.K. But she seemed to go every which way at once. She sure is a beautiful dog. I would have hated to hurt her."

"Oh, Mandy, if anything had happened to you . . ."

Mandy sensed she had come very close to a bad end. She left Sam's lap where she had sprawled like a large rug, and tucked herself tightly under her chair.

"You be careful from now on, you hear." The man bent down and waved his finger at Mandy. Mandy's tail thumped an uncertain answer. She was in no mood to make new friends or to establish a relationship. Her head stayed tucked in between her paws.

They watched him pull away. Neither Sam nor Sue spoke for quite a while. Sue leaned on the back of the wheelchair, while Sam sat in front of her, locked in her own thoughts.

"She's all I have," Sam said at last. Her voice sounded so weak, as if all her barriers had crumbled away on that quiet street but moments before. "She's my best friend."

Sue walked to the front of Sam's wheelchair and faced her. "You're lucky to have a good friend like Mandy."

"Besides Mandy, I've never really had a best friend." Then she looked up at Sue. "I'm not even sure what it takes to be a good friend."

"It takes giving . . . and I guess accepting. Yes, I guess when you're friends, you have to accept one another's help."

"I don't accept help easily," Sam said firmly.

"Neither do I." Sue kneeled down in front of Sam, facing her directly, so that Sam's eyes had nowhere to go but straight ahead. "Sam, I want to be able to help you when you have to use our toilets." There, it was out. Words like bits of sand tossed in the wind. She couldn't get them back, even if she wanted to. She didn't want to.

Sam shifted in her chair. "I'm not sure that I need help."

"Yes, you do," Sue yelled, losing her patience. "I know you need help. I know it must be hard for you. Johnny Jay isn't going to change things today, not for a while, if ever. I want you to teach me how to lift you. And I want you to know that I am available to help you whenever you need it. I want that understood now." Her voice matched Sam's in firmness. "If we're to be friends, then I want to give. I can't have a friendship without giving."

The hands in the bright blue sweat suit twisted in Sam's lap. There were no doors between them now. Mandy's mad dash, her close brush with death, had waved away all the games, and now there was this urgent need to say what must be said and let the reactions fall where they may.

"It's not the greatest solution, not the one you really should have," Sue went on breathlessly, "but, Sam, don't ruin your health. Don't endanger yourself because of some silly pride. Let me help you until things are right."

She waited, knowing Sam's decision would be the turning point in their relationship.

"O.K.," Sam said at last. "If I need you, I promise I'll ask for your help. And I will teach you how to lift me." Her smile was warm as she added, "Thanks for wanting to know."

They sat there for a while, Sue on the ground beside the wheelchair, Sam thoughtfully stroking Mandy, who sat propped up on her hind legs, her front paws and head resting in Sam's lap.

The three of them then continued their journey toward Heartbreak Hill. Mandy dutifully stayed at the edge of Sam's elbow, not caring to remember her impetuous adventure into the outside world.

"There it is," Sue said at last. The three of them looked up. Ahead of them, winding arrogantly upward for over a mile ahead was a crooked, bumpy pavement. "It rises over a hundred and forty feet," said Sue. She felt its ominous power more than ever. "So many runners will be beaten by the time they reach this point." She looked toward Sam.

"But we're not beaten now." Sam was staring up the hill, her eyes filled with a new kind of wonder.

"No, we're not," Sue said. And so they started upward slowly. Sam's wheelchair dipped into the cracks, bumping precariously over the pavement.

Sue wanted to reach out and steady her friend's chair, but she knew she dared not. She heard Sam's grunts, saw her mouth clamp tight, fighting against the incessant height of the hill. Slowly, with an even pace, they crept up it, the hill allowing them but inches at a time. Mandy was the only one not having trouble. She kept close to Sam's side though, remembering where curiosity had taken her before.

Now and then Sam would look back. Below them now was the greater part of the hill and the town which sat like a gathering of toy logs, trees barren, as if someone had forgotten to dot them with leaves. Streets glistened in the early-morning sun.

"The marathon goes through it all," Sue said breathlessly, "cracks and potholes, rail tracks, the works. We expect to have over a thousand runners. You know," she confided, "sometimes when I run, I get kite-like feelings, as if I'm up there," she pointed to the sky, "floating somewhere."

"That must be a great feeling." Sam was moving slower now, but her pace was constant. She was looking ahead, toward the top of the hill.

"It's steep. It's even steeper than it looks." Sam's words were coming between deep breaths, almost as if she were digging down for every new thrust of strength.

"We're nearly there," Sue encouraged her.

The top of the hill was now just an arm's distance away. Sam gave the wheels one long thrust and it pushed her over the top. She let out a victorious shout, throwing her arms up in the air, "Just a few months ago, I couldn't even make it up the hill in the parking space of the animal shelter," she said, and then proudly, "but look what I can do now."

"That's what working out is all about." Sue stood there watching Sam enjoy the victory of the climb. Below them stretched the hill, now submissive, now conquered.

"It's a tough hill," Sue reminded her, "and much tougher after you've done miles and miles." It was as if she were warning her, giving her one last moment to reconsider what they both knew had already been decided.

"The potholes, the bumps, were new to me this time. But next time, I'll know better how to manage them."

Samantha wheeled around the track which circled the hill's peak. Mandy paced beside her, back and forth. "It would be a great hill to conquer in a marathon," Sam said, smiling.

"I know."

"I want to go up it again."

"We will," Sue assured her.

"And again," Sam turned to her, the walls forever down between them. Trust was there. "Until the April marathon, and then I want to go up it that one last time, after the seventeen miles."

Mandy looked over sharply as if she caught the words and didn't quite approve. Perhaps she was considering her own involvement in running the route of the Marathon.

"Will you help me enter the marathon? Will you help me train for it?" Sam asked.

It didn't take long for the answer to come. Sue's words echoed right down Heartbreak Hill and even past it.

"You bet I will," she shouted.

6 ───────

"I didn't know you were such a great bowler." Johnny looked her way as the pins collapsed one atop the other.

"I didn't either." Lately she was surprised by a lot of things she did unexpectedly. Johnny entering her life and staying was the biggest surprise of all. One day he had just met her after class and asked her to drive home with him. It had caught her by surprise. She had said yes. Without saying it would happen every day, it seemed to be doing just that. He was usually waiting outside her class when the bell rang. Mandy knew him so well now, that she ran to greet him, giving him one of the face washings that she saved for special people.

Samantha found herself looking for his face during the day, for the shock of red hair. She noticed she felt much better whenever she could get a chance to glance his way, or even have a moment in between classes to exchange a few words. Though they usually found more than they needed to talk about, there was one subject that neither trespassed on, though it still hung there silently between them. It was Johnny's circus, as Samantha often thought of it, his moments pacing in front of the toilet. She avoided him when he was there. He kept his signs out of her sight when they drove home.

Other than that, she felt as if they were two navigators exploring a new relationship.

"I can't even think of any advice to give you to make your game better."

"Coming from you that's something," she joked.

He looked her way and smiled. She liked what she saw in his face. She felt he must be seeing the same thing in her eyes.

They were in the last frame. Now and then she caught him taking a quick glance at his watch. Her bowling ball left three pins standing.

"Have someplace to go?" she asked, getting a spare, then a strike, and winding up the game with a victorious shout.

They had chosen Saturday morning because the lanes were fairly empty. She had hoped perhaps they might have the entire day together.

A couple of months ago, she would have thought it impossible that she would want an entire day with Johnny. Five minutes of exposure to his project in the hallway had been enough for her. But he had inched up on her, and she found that his excitement about living spilled over on many of the things she enjoyed. Bowling. Ping-Pong. He had a table in his house. Movies. They both loved all types and popcorn with it. The museum. She hadn't been there in so long, she forgave him when he caused a scene when they couldn't get past the front steps. They both went up to the second floor on a freight elevator. She didn't mind. She felt they must have looked pretty funny, stuffed in with all the boxes. He fumed all the way up, and all the way down.

Perhaps it was that unpredictability that excited her. He was a small pressure cooker with the steam always shooting out. Instead of getting her angry now, it made her laugh. There was no end to his energy and no stopping his campaigns.

"You should get your own bowling ball, Sam." He helped her on with her coat.

"I never really thought about bowling on a regular basis before. But maybe I will. I enjoy beating the hide off of you."

"Enjoy it while you can, lady. I don't intend to let it happen forever."

They were in the car, still parked, when he drew her to him and kissed her. She didn't pull away. She surprised herself by kissing him back. It felt so good she didn't want to stop.

"You look terrific today," he said. "I love you in blue." He touched her sweater. She flushed. "But you always look terrific." He murmured it into her hair. "Sometimes I just rush around school trying to get one good look at you before the day begins."

She snuggled into his arms. She knew she did the same. But she didn't quite feel like letting him know that yet.

"It makes the day better, you know what I mean. Just one special face. Now I keep wondering how I began the day before without seeing that face. You're a habit, that's what you are." His arms grew tighter, and then, "I saw you with Ms. Jenkins the other day. Looks like you two were working out. That's a great sweat suit you were wearing."

She nodded under his chin. "We were working out."

"For what?" He drew her face up again toward his and kissed her on the nose. "Remind me to tell you sometime how terrific I think your nose is. Do you know it tilts up just at the end?"

"The Heartbreak Hill Marathon. I'm going to compete."

"Hey," he swept her close to him, his pride reaching out, "you tiger . . . you little tiger." He threw his head back, the smile touching every part of his face. "You are great. You are just great," he said, over and over while he playfully chided her and she punched him lightly to break loose.

"That's some challenge," he said more seriously later as they pulled away from the lot.

"I know. But I feel I have to do it."

He took her hand in his. "I know," he said

thoughtfully. "I guess each of us has our own Heartbreak Hill. Once you find it, you have to go up it, or you'll never know if you could."

She knew he was talking about the toilets. She didn't continue the conversation.

"Where are we going?" She had her arms looped under his elbow and leaned contentedly against his rough jacket. For the first time, she noticed the day held dark, wintry storm clouds. Often when she was with him, there didn't even seem time to notice the weather.

"I have an errand to go on," he answered, but his voice had taken on a sudden seriousness. He looked at her for a quick moment, and there was concern in his eyes. "I think you should go with me." The air of authority was there. She still felt warmed by his kisses. The two combined made her feel wanted and loved.

Sam sat back, missing the big furry body that usually squeezed itself between them on their after-school rides home. Mandy had not liked being left home. She sat sulking by the front door, a very forlorn expression on her face as Johnny explained patiently to her that there are some places a working dog does not have to go, and furthermore, he would very definitely take good care of Sam, and besides, even dogs need a day off just to lie back and relax. He petted Mandy lovingly, making sure that he didn't endanger the relationship that he had so carefully established. Both he and Sam knew if Mandy didn't approve of Johnny, there would be no getting her in the car.

Mandy had stayed behind reluctantly. But even though she stood wistfully, following them out the door with her eyes, Sam turned to see her curl up in front of the fireplace on the mat, as if indeed her day off would be eagerly accepted.

Johnny grew very quiet as they drove through the Saturday early-afternoon shoppers into the middle of the city. Samantha took this unusual lapse in his talkative mood to tell him about her training, and how she was getting stronger and stronger. Sue Jenkins had sent away for applications for both of them to fill out and return to the marathon committee.

"I think I'll keep running, even after the marathon," Sam said, almost to herself. "I look forward to it each day. And I feel better. Sue said that I could keep entering wherever marathons are held. I could travel to New York or Massachusetts; there's a big one there every year."

Johnny slowed the car down and pulled over carefully. "There doesn't seem to be any handicapped parking around here," he said. She knew he was making a mental note to follow it up with a letter of protest to the city. Once they had gone shopping in a nearby mall. There had been a section set up for handicapped parking. It was an especially large parking area that enabled them to get out their wheelchairs, but there was a car already filling the space. The car parked there didn't have a handicapped parking permit on the front window. She had stayed uncomfortably by his side while Johnny flagged down a police car and remained until the policeman had placed a ticket on the windshield of the car.

"So we can park over there." Sam pointed to a space near a meter. "Does it matter?"

"It'll matter someday to you when you drive and you're stuck between two cars and you can't get out of your own car. Then it'll matter a lot." He sometimes grew cross with her when she tried to calm him. He'd call her apathetic. Other times passive. She'd call him unreasonable. Sometimes fanatic. But they never stayed angry for long.

"We can park here. It's still a couple of blocks away. O.K. with you?"

"Sure."

Samantha pulled her wheelchair from the back seat. It was so much easier for her now to transfer and to take care of herself in situations that had been difficult for her before. Her arms had gained an added strength from working out. She pulled herself out of the front seat and into the chair. Carefully she adjusted her skirt, folding her heavy winter coat over her knees, buttoning the top button of the fur around her collar. She moved away from the car, allowing Johnny room to get out. He also came out on the passenger's side. It was much easier for him, he had explained to her once, to transfer away from the steering wheel. It gave him more room to manipulate the chair out of the back seat of the car.

Johnny put some money in the parking meter and they made their way up the busy city street. Samantha now and then stopped, gazing into the beautiful large store windows. The spring clothes already being displayed in the store windows reminded her that April was not too far away. She felt the chill of the raw wind around her, and welcomed the touch of spring filling up the large department store display cases.

Johnny rushed down the street ahead of her. He was constantly a half block ahead, now and then turning around to keep track of what she was doing, motioning her on when she got involved with the street stalls spilling over with jewelry. She enjoyed trying on the necklaces, the rings, rummaging through the scarfs and gay hats.

They stopped for a hamburger. He put mustard on his. She ate hers without. He liked everything seasoned. She liked it plain.

"I'm glad you came," he said as she finally caught up with him.

"I'm glad I came, too. Even though I don't know where we're going." He liked to keep their day a surprise. Sometimes he'd just say, "Wear something sporty," or, "It's dress-up time," and they'd go somewhere flashy for dinner. But now and then, they'd both dress up to the teeth, he with a dinner jacket, she with a long shirt and tight-fitting jersey, and long silvery earrings.

Through the good times, as he became more and more a part of her life, she would see her father's worried face in the background. He had never said another word about Johnny, not one more word of disapproval, when Johnny began dropping her off after school. Then picking her up to go to school. Then showing up on Saturdays and sometimes Sundays, whenever she wasn't working out. But the edginess was there, that something hesitant that she could see working through her father's face as if everything was quiet, but nothing was settled. "That boy will bring up trouble." She remembered her father's words. She looked over at Johnny, his cheeks red from the winter wind, the nose straight, as if it knew just where to stop, above a mouth that could be as warm as it could be determined. He didn't look as if he could bring trouble to anyone. She wanted to tell her father that. Maybe, if Johnny and she continued seeing each other, she would. Maybe one night she would just sit down and open up her mind to her father. She felt she could do that now. Johnny had taught that. He wouldn't let her keep a latch on her feelings or her thoughts. "Come on, Sam," he'd urge her, 'let's get it out in the open. If something's bothering you, don't keep it to yourself. Let me in on it." And she had. Time and time again. Until letting her feelings be known had seemed as natural as conquering Heartbreak Hill. She liked to feel it would be that easy. One by one, he had unlatched door after door, encouraging her to speak out, to explain what she so often held inside. He had convinced her it was much better that way.

The rain came on them suddenly and the wind curled around the corner as Johnny wheeled toward a large crowd in front of the Federal building. Samantha followed, eager to get out of the storm that suddenly had taken on a renewed force. With her head bent down slightly, she followed Johnny's wheels, not daring to look up and be faced with the sharp wind that cut at her breath and flung her coat open. Then they were under the shelter of the building. Samantha saw a large sign sticking up from the crowd: **County Alliance for the Blind.**

A man was standing in the middle of the crowd, on a small platform, a Seeing Eye dog standing next to him. The wind was no match for his words as they carried down the several hundred feet to where Johnny and Samantha sat. "We need these SSI allowances to live, and we need them now. We cannot put up with the red tape, a failing computer system, an indifferent bureaucracy, and a bureau that doesn't seem to be listening to anybody. The blind, the elderly, the physically disabled cannot afford to do without their money while this bureau tries to reorganize its mailing."

"What's going on here, Johnny?" Sam looked around her, confused. And then dumbfounded, she realized aloud, "This is a demonstration. You've brought me to a demonstration."

The speaker's voice blotted out her own. "Many blind people have been receiving no money at all," he went on. "New mailing addresses have not been followed up. We hope that when our plight becomes known, the public will demand that SSI correct its system and give blind people the fair treatment they deserve. With millions of people in one computer system, checks are sent out randomly to wrong parts of the country while those who are blind and dependent go without money to pay their rent, food bills, and living expenses."

"You lied to me. You said you had an errand to do." Samantha tugged at his arm, pulling him away from the crowd.

"This is my errand. They need bodies here today. Numbers to show power and support. I promised them I'd show up and bring as many people as I could. The more people milling around here, the better it will look and maybe the sooner this whole thing will get cleared up."

Sam's eyes blazed. "How dare you involve me. How dare you! You know how I feel about this kind of thing."

"Come on, Sam," he tried to calm her down, "loosen up. Don't make such a big deal out of it. We'll just stay a little while. Everyone here is fighting for something that might eventually affect you. They need our help."

"But I don't know what they're fighting for, and I don't care. Oh, you're impossible." She turned away from him, feeling trapped, knowing that until he decided to go, there was no going for her either.

"SSI," he stubbornly tried to explain, "means Supplementary Security Income. It's for those who can't work because they're disabled. Their money is being held up, and we're down here protesting it."

She looked at him accusingly. "You knew all the

time, even while we were bowling. You knew when you asked me out today."

"Now hold it. One thing has nothing to do with the other." He matched her anger now, as they sat huddled together, faces close to each other as the crowd around them grew noisier. "I wanted to take you out today. The fact that I had something important to take care of and didn't really feel it would make such a dent in you . . . that was secondary. Probably my biggest mistake was in thinking you would understand."

She turned away from him and faced a blind man who didn't even know she was there because of the confusion around them. Johnny always had a way of throwing guilt into her lap. Well, today, she would throw it back. "No it's you who doesn't understand."

"Look, I'll be right back," Johnny said softly to the back of her.

"Go. I don't care where you go. Just don't make me go along."

She sat there listening to the incessant demands of the speakers, one after the other, as the cold winter winds picked up strength and set the protesters to pulling up their coat collars. She would get pneumonia, out in this weather, and for what? For a bunch of people she didn't know. For something called SSI that she didn't even understand. She hoped that perhaps, as the weather grew more violent, the crowd would disperse. The rain was beginning to whip under the small shelter. No one seemed to notice it. Some sang softly. Some huddled under umbrellas. Others took their places on the platform and one speech followed another.

Samantha looked up at the blind man. Unless she said something to him, he would probably never even know she existed. There were too many people on either side of him pushing every way for him to sense her presence. Thinking about that took her mind off the cold and the dark, wet strings of hair that hung over her coat. She closed her eyes for a moment, and tried to imagine what the man standing in front of her must be seeing, or not seeing. Even with her eyes closed, she saw a brightness. She wondered if there was any light cutting through his darkness. Or was it just that. Black. She tried to imagine the earth without light, the sky above without its blue, but merely something overhead that dropped such things as rain and snow and heat. She opened her eyes. The light hurt them for a moment.

Pretending to be blind was not being blind. It was the same with wheelchairs. Some people were getting in chairs for the day, and going about their jobs, just to feel what Sam felt every day. It seemed like a harmless enough game to her. They could pretend. But they would never know. As long as they knew that they could get up and walk to the water fountain if they had to, or if they got tired pushing, just stop. Just as she knew she could open her eyes. With some things, there was just no pretending.

Sam knew it was Johnny's touch on her shoulder even before she turned around.

"We are not receiving adequate monthly benefits now. Some of us who are not receiving money will have no place to live soon." The wind picked up the speaker's words and sent them her way. The crowd was still growing.

"I'm sorry," Johnny said. "I should have told you where we were going. I guess it really wasn't fair."

She didn't have time to accept his apology. A large truck pulled up. A sign identifying it as representing a local TV station was attached to the hood of the van. A man with a microphone jumped off. He worked his way through the crowd as a cameraman followed behind him.

Samantha and Johnny watched fascinated as the microphone found its way to the speaker who directed his remarks into the camera, and then wound its way toward a blind person who stood under an umbrella, his dog huddled wetly beside him.

Johnny's arm still clung protectively to Sam's shoulder. It felt warm, even through her coat, and with the chill of the winter winds, she welcomed it in spite of her anger. She nestled toward him, her shivering body looking for any shelter it might find.

"We'll leave in a couple of minutes," he said. "This is what we wanted. The attention of the media. Now everyone will have to listen. This is what we came for."

Samantha shrugged. She was too wet and tired to argue. The anger was still burning in her. She still had plenty left to say to him about today, but it could wait. They were leaving shortly and that was all she needed to know for the moment.

And then the cameramen were coming toward them, even as she watched, horrified, and wanted to turn and run away, if there had been room to run. She saw the man with the microphone look her way, and then look again and smile. And then they were moving toward her, the men with the earphones, and the long wires, and the camera being carried, and the microphone, each connected with the other by wires and plugs and lights. It was as if she could see the idea bursting in the newsman's head as he looked her way.

"Hello," said the reporter. He looked familiar. She recognized him as the anchorman from the evening news. His voice was mellow, deep, smooth.

"Hi," Johnny answered eagerly, shaking his hand. Samantha smiled weakly.

"Let's go," she whispered to Johnny. "Come on, please, let's get out of here."

But the microphone already held Johnny in its spell. He didn't see the pleading in Sam's eyes. The excitement of being interviewed on television was all he had room for. Samantha sat there helplessly, remembering her father's words . . . his worry over holding his job. What would he do, what would be the repercussions if she were to appear on TV in a demonstration in front of the Federal building?

"How did it happen you came down here?" the interviewer asked. The microphone was pointed toward Johnny, the camera toward the both of them. "Isn't this an issue being raised by the blind?"

Johnny's eyes shone with a special brilliance as he answered, "It's everyone's issue. We're joining together now. Last month when we were fighting the transit system for accessible buses, the blind supported us."

Samantha felt the heat of the cameras and lights. They were still clicking her way, forming a net around her. She knew there was no escaping now. The reporter was obviously delighted with his find. How sweet they must have looked, both of them in wheelchairs, Johnny's arm still around her, she wet and shivering, accepting his arm as shelter when actually at the moment she would have preferred to rip him in two.

"And you, miss. You must feel the same way. You must have very strong convictions about all this, to stay out here in such terrible weather."

Before she could answer, though no clear answer had come to mind, the cameras accepted her silence as a yes, and went on their way to seek out another interview. The news reporter called out just before he disappeared into the crowd, "You'll be on the six o'clock news tonight." It seemed they had won a prize.

A hush suddenly fell over the crowd. It was as if even the rain was holding back now, slowing to a drizzle. A man with a rain hat on, his body hunched as if he were very tired, stepped onto the small platform.

"I will personally see to it that all of your complaints are answered within thirty days. I shall report to the different groups represented in this crowd and to the press during those thirty days so that you are aware of what this bureau is doing." He ended his statement with a wave to the crowd. The man was an official representing the government.

A loud cheer, an ocean of victory, swept through the crowd which joined together in a large embrace.

Samantha didn't cheer along with them. She didn't feel as if it were her victory. But more than that, she felt she had been used, brought here just as an added body that was needed to fill in a crowd. Johnny had brought her, and in doing that, had used her.

She sat there watching Johnny and his friends celebrate. But all she could think of was the six o'clock news and her father, who would be watching, and the school administration, some of whom would be watching.

She knew now she must not allow herself to be put in this position a second time. The only way to guarantee it was to stay away from Johnny, to stay far away . . . and never to allow herself to be used again.

7 ——————

Johnny sat in his car in front of the school and waited. Every couple of minutes he would nervously check his watch. Now and then he would look out the window, first to the side, then checking the back.

They would be here soon. Then it would all be out in the open. No more meetings behind closed doors. No more board meetings and staff meetings. Weeks and weeks of planning would finally come together in Johnny's finally answering their silence.

The members of NOD and the blind coalition had promised their support. Through all the days of mapping out their strategy, through the poster making, through the repeated discussions regarding the way it should be handled, they had said, in numbers, they would be there.

It was difficult, keeping it in, walking around in school every day knowing what was soon to happen. But there was no one in school he could trust to share it with.

Not even Samantha. Perhaps Samantha least of all. He checked the signs propped on his wheelchair in the back seat. They were all there.

Samantha. His hands tightened around the steering wheel. The brown eyes took on a lost look. She had shut him off . . . from that moment in front of the Federal building when she had accused him of using her. Then later that night, when he tried to ring, hoping that if they talked about it she might understand, Samantha had again shut him off, jamming the telephone down on his ear. Everyday since then, she made U turns around him. If she wanted him to beg, to run after her, she wanted something he couldn't give her. He'd give her anything else she wanted. He felt that way about her. He had from the start. From the moment he had seen those eyes dominating her sensitive face, from the moment he had watched her graceful hands etch out a story as she spoke, he knew. But now she didn't believe him. She believed he wanted only her support in what he was doing.

He couldn't deny that was partly true. Sitting there, waiting for perhaps what would be one of the most important moments of his life, he would have liked to have her near him, there in the car, making the waiting easier.

He was well aware of how hard it was to bring

someone who didn't believe into your camp. He had plenty of experience. Scot High had provided him that. No one there could seem to find the necessary money to make the alterations on the toilets. Everyone was caught up in legalities, and paperwork, and board meetings that were called off and rescheduled.

Change. The hardest thing in life to do. Change a mind. It was like moving a million preformed opinions from one head to another. Changing a building seemed the most difficult thing of all.

He didn't realize there were so many people who had fears about it. Lately the opinions were finding their way to him. Some people in the town were afraid of taxes being raised because of increased building expenses at the school. Others were afraid that the tuition in local colleges might have to be raised to make allowances for accessibility spending. Most of all was the confusion among the teaching staff. At the meetings Johnny was allowed to attend, the question seemed to be how the teachers were to come to terms with the large number of new students with new problems. The solving of each new problem would mean money. More and more money. One teacher from another school had made the comment, "Our school isn't accessible. But that's O.K. We don't have any handicapped students going to it." Johnny might have laughed if the statement hadn't been so pathetic. There were no handicapped students because they couldn't get into the school.

Only last week, NOD members had spoken at the meeting of a workshop where people who came were given assigments from the disabled. The able-bodied were told to get a cold drink from the machine on the fifth floor (in a wheelchair). Buy a newspaper at the hotel across the street (blindfolded). Bring back the towel from the rack above the toilet in your room (in a wheelchair). Get a candy bar from a concession stand in the lobby (on crutches). Make a call from the pay phone outside the hotel (using a walker). Those brave enough to experiment stretched, reached, stumbled, were stared at, and in general got a taste of the world of the disabled, his world. But it was just a taste. Some would remember. Some would forget.

He couldn't do that. Johnny lay his head back on the seat cushion behind him. He needed all the help he could get. For just this toilet, for both the toilets, for Sam's toilet, too. He needed her help, her voice, her talent in writing. He needed her words to slam a powerful hammer down toward the administration.

He had tried the past week to break through that screen Sam had put in front of her. He knew what that screen stood for, and if at some time she didn't let it down, it would ruin her life. Each time she passed him without speaking, she was stating, "You're disabled. Not I. I'm just the way I was years ago. You need to be with disabled people. I don't."

She infuriated him with those blue eyes that

could chill him when they looked his way. Johnny rolled his window down and peered up the street. Cars were beginning to pull into the parking area.

What if they didn't show? What if they changed their minds? It was their first active sit-in in a school. Johnny knew many of them had transportation problems and would have to get rides. Others might just be frightened at taking such a forceful step.

But they had agreed. It had been unanimous at the NOD meeting. Meeting after meeting, they had taken counts. Vote after vote had gone his way. It was the only way left open to them. Letters to members of the school board from NOD had brought polite rebuttals and stalling tactics. A personal discussion with the principal had brought confusion and no results.

They now knew that only their bodies in number would bring some recognition of their problem. Though there were only two disabled in the school, one of whom didn't want to think of herself as disabled, there was always the possibility of more disabled entering. With the law now opening up education, there would be more and more disabled students wanting to take courses. More and more would want to get into the washrooms.

NOD had decided to use Johnny's case as one that would establish a precedent. Now, sitting there with the cars filling up the parking spaces, Johnny felt the enormous responsibility of what they were about to do. He knew the possible repercussion. He could get expelled. They all could get arrested. It could happen. All who had agreed to come agreed to the options that might follow.

It would be peaceful. That was agreed upon from the beginning. They would cause no violence, no destruction. They would just sit, give out information, and try to get the attention of the administration. He thought again of good-old-not-needing-anyone Samantha Lee Anderson. She would probably stay as far away as she could. He didn't care. He felt if he said it often enough, he wouldn't care.

A car pulled up beside Johnny's. A crutch stood up like a wooden soldier in the passenger side. The driver leaned over to where Johnny could see him. "Hey, Johnny, lead the way. Where do we park?" Jim Muller asked. Johnny looked back, behind Jim's car. Lined up like a parade was one car after another. Each car had a symbol-of-access sticker on its front window and a handicapped driver's notice on the plates. Johnny started his car and led the assembly of cars to the back of the school where there was a large parking space still empty.

His army of disabled began to unpack their wheelchairs, and unload their Seeing Eye dogs. Some had helpers to push their chairs. Most came alone.

When all were out of the cars, a small circle formed around Johnny. Altogether, there were about twenty wheelchairs with helpers and signs. It seemed like much more. Wheelchairs had a way of filling up a room.

There were an odd assortment of people gathered together and they quickly attracted the attention of students passing by. Footsteps around them slowed down, heads turned, some fellow students even stopped to find out what was happening. No one told them too much.

The president of NOD stopped the social gathering abruptly as she said, "O.K., let's get started."

Johnny led the way, the wheelchairs and dogs and signs and helpers following. He led them to the main hallway where the toilets sat waiting, as if today they knew they would be the focus of attention.

Silently, quietly, the signs were posted along the walls, propped up, some with bold red lettering, some black and white. The signs spoke for themselves.

We want our education. We need accessibility. How many toilets can't you get into?

It's taken us over three years to push the bill into law. We can't wait three years to get into this toilet.

"Look, I've got classes to go to," Johnny said.

"Don't miss them." A boy about nineteen waved him on. "We'll keep things going here."

Johnny didn't hear a thing Ms. Jenkins said in English class. His ears were tuned to the comments coming from the students as they walked into class.

Johnny joined the group gathered in the front of the toilets during each of his breaks. There was always a crowd now milling about, reading the signs, talking to the members of NOD, picking up pieces of literature that lay on a nearby table. During lunch, he took his place beside them.

"Has any one of the teachers come up to you?" Johnny asked one of the demonstrators.

"No, they just keep looking us over, and there seems to be a lot of activity in that office down the hall." He pointed to the principal's office. Only last week, in that very same office, the principal had cautioned him, "Johnny, we can't do everything at once. Change takes time."

That's when Johnny knew they had to speed up the clock. The hall was now filled with the curious who stopped to encourage them on. Only Samantha didn't stop. Only she with her head held high, her eyes still hot with an anger he couldn't cope with, only she, glancing quickly his way, then off in another direction, wheeled past them as if they didn't exist.

Though they stayed throughout the day, nothing happened. No one came out of the office to speak with them. It was a silence that disturbed them, as if their presence were not even being recognized. But they were prepared for that reaction. The school staff was riding the day out, as one would ride out an unpleasant cold. Only Sue Jenkins came over toward the end of the day.

"How's it going?" she asked Johnny.

"We won't know for a while," he answered.

She squeezed his hand. "Don't give up," she whispered. Give up? The possibility hadn't entered his mind. He had to get into the toilet. It wasn't a matter of victory or defeat. It was a matter of necessity. He didn't know any other way he could continue at this school or any school if this problem persisted. He watched her run down the hall and corner Sam in front of the English class.

And then he read a series of expressions on Sam's face that both worried and frightened him. First he saw surprise, Sam's large eyes opening wide. Then disappointment filled those eyes as she bent her head down. And then he saw despair, as Sam's hands covered her face. Ms. Jenkins seemed to be trying to calm her but Sam kept shaking her head. In that moment, Johnny wanted to run to her. And then she looked up. And he saw in Sam's eyes a fierceness he had never expected to see there.

The bell rang, bringing the day to a close. The halls filled with students rushing out of classes. He lost sight of Sam. The NOD group picked up their signs and assembled in a group outside the school in the parking area. It was decided to come back the next day. Everyone there agreed that to leave today would be saying nothing. Not until someone from the administration sat down and discussed the problem that existed and how it could be solved. So they would come back tomorrow, and the day after if necessary, and the day after that. Until some action was taken.

The next day started the same way, with everyone meeting in the parking area and then proceeding to the middle hallway—in front of the toilets, which now claimed a unique kind of fame.

"I'll stay with you here this morning," Johnny told Jim Muller. He had an intuitive feeling that something was going to happen. He wanted to be there when it did.

The first hours went by slowly. The same faces moved past them, smiling and waving now. Some stopped to talk to those with whom they had begun to get friendly from the day before. Two hours passed, then three. Then suddenly the main office door opened wide, as if to make way for a procession of people. The principal of the school came out first. Next came a couple of teachers. And then two policemen followed. Johnny's hands tightened. They had talked about this possibility and they knew what to do. But the reality of it was much more traumatic than he had expected. He felt his stomach circle around on its own private merry-go-round. The procession of people filed toward them.

"Johnny," the principal addressed him, as if he were informing him of a tragedy in his family, "Johnny, you and your friends will have to leave now. This is private property and your friends are trespassing. We will have to try to find another way to handle this problem, but this isn't the way, I assure you."

"Before we leave, there are some things we should discuss with you." The president of NOD came forward.

But Johnny could tell by the principal's face that the discussion had closed.

"You'd better all break up now," one of the policemen urged.

"O.K., pack it up," the president ordered quietly. It had been agreed upon. They were like actors on a stage, each knowing his or her part. The blind led their dogs away. Some carried signs tucked under their arms.

The wheelchairs rolled softly out through the front doorway while many of the students began to gather around the thinning band of demonstrators.

One by one, Johnny saw his army retreat. But it wasn't really a retreat. In his heart, he knew that. They had agreed that if ordered they would leave, all of them would leave, but Johnny. For then, and only then, was it his battle alone. He would represent their vote and their numbers. He would be the last to hold on to the Alamo. Just a few signs remained propped up against the walls. His signs.

Then he was there alone. The hall was now empty of the NOD members, but filled with a fairly large crowd from school. The policemen and the principal faced him. Thinking about what he would do in this situation, spouting bravely in front of the NOD meetings, was much different from the actuality of the confrontation. They were waiting for him to leave, too.

Instead he took one of the signs leaning against the wall and began his familiar pace back and forth in front of the toilet. There was a loud wave of applause from his fellow students.

"Johnny, I've put up with this, with your private crusade here, for months. It ends now," the principal said firmly. "You will have to find another way to deal with the situation. I told you the school board will be considering your complaints, but we must have time."

"How much time?" Johnny asked.

"I won't discuss it with you here and now. I can't promise you anything. All I can say is that we'll try."

Johnny sat there feeling the eyes of the students concentrating in his direction. They were waiting for his answer. It wasn't his private crusade. How could the principal think that? He was fighting for the hundreds of students who weren't even born yet.

Only the hall clock dared to utter a sound. All else seemed to have gulped in one deep breath, without letting it out.

"I can't leave," Johnny said at last. "Just like I can't get into there." He pointed to the large letters . . . **BOYS.**

"I will not allow any student of this school to behave in this manner," the principal said sternly. "I will not condone this type of protest. You are expelled for two weeks. And if you come back to continue this disturbance to the school routine, you will be expelled for the rest of the year."

They each had finally made their stand. Instead of the sickening politeness of the past months, there was now at least the comfort of honesty. They both had something to defend. Johnny wasn't denying that. They each had the right to defend it.

"I'll assist you from the building," the policeman said, looking as if it were the last thing he wanted to do.

"I can leave myself." Johnny released the brakes on his wheelchair, gathered up the remaining signs, put them on his lap, and wheeled past the crowd. As he went, he felt hands softly touch his shoulder.

"That'a a boy, Johnny."

"We're with you, Johnny."

"Don't give up the fight, Johnny."

Over and over again. His fellow students knew what he meant . . . they finally understood what he was fighting for. At least he had succeeded in that. He felt warmed by their support, but a sense of defeat came along with it. Now expelled for two weeks, there would be no one to remind them. People had a way of forgetting quickly.

And then he saw Samantha's face. Samantha, tears coming out of those wide blue eyes, streaking down her cheeks. She reached out. He touched her hand, then both held on tightly for a long moment, as if sealing a silent pledge.

And then he knew . . . in that moment when hands clutched, he had passed it to her . . . and she had accepted it. She would carry on where he left off.

8 ——————

She knew what she had to do the moment her hand touched his. The timing had a touch of irony to it. She was on her way to ask him for advice . . . for help. Sue Jenkins had dropped a bomb in her lap.

The marathon committee wouldn't let Samantha compete in the spring marathon. It had rejected her application, with a kind note explaining it was only for her own good.

"They were afraid you or the other runners might get hurt," Sue had tried to explain yesterday in the hallway.

Sam had felt as if someone had thrust a fist in her stomach. After all the weeks and months of training, after repeated trial runs up Heartbreak Hill, they were turning her away.

No. That simply, they had said no. She found

herself not being able to accept their answer. She
wanted to compete in the Heartbreak Hill Marathon more than anything she had ever wanted in
her life. It was more than the hill. It had something to do with seeing a challenge in front of her,
that spoke to her, that was pointing its finger in
her direction. She was good. She knew it. She had
endurance. The workouts had been tough. Sue
had seen to it that she regulated her diet, was getting plenty of sleep. Her life had begun to revolve
around that moment in the spring.

And they had said no. Because the members of
the marathon committee thought they knew what
would happen. Though they couldn't be sure,
unless they had documented proof that someone
somewhere had been injured, or had injured
someone else because of their wheelchair. The
committee members felt they were protecting her,
or themselves. She couldn't figure out which. But
all of a sudden she understood the pounding in
Johnny that wouldn't let him let go of his signs.
She couldn't let go now of what she wanted, either. She would do anything to change the decision.

She had been on her way to ask Johnny for his
help, when she heard the principal expel him.
Sam felt in that moment that part of her had been
expelled, too. Johnny had received the blow. She
felt his pain.

They had to help one another. Sam knew that
now. Alone, she didn't stand a chance against the

committee. But perhaps, with the support of NOD and Johnny, perhaps they could enlighten the committee as to what must be done in order for her to compete.

"Mandy, get me my notebook. . . . Notebook, Mandy!"

Mandy yawned, stretching her long legs across the bedroom rug. She shook the sleep out of her body, then walked over to the notebook sticking up from Sam's schoolbag. Carefully, she picked it up between her teeth and carried it back to Sam.

"Good girl." Sam rubbed Mandy behind the ears, then placed the notebook on the desk in front of her. Mandy took her place back on the throw rug, her eyes slowly drooping closed again.

Samantha knew she would have to fill the pages of the book in front of her with words that would help Johnny.

The touch of his hand had told her that. He was passing it to her. What she did with it would be for him, for her, for others. It was the others Johnny had always spoken about. She had never seen them before. Johnny had seen them. Just as she was seeing now that if she couldn't compete in April, neither could anyone else in a wheelchair who might come after her, next year or the year after, and who might want to try. But if she paved the way, if she opened the door, it would stay open.

Johnny had been trying to tell her that all along. She had to fight for the disabled because she was one of them. Samantha, she said to herself, you are never going to walk again. You are never going to climb steps, be able to reach a high water fountain, make a call in a phone booth without some adjustments. You're never going to walk, and that's that, baby. It didn't feel as bad as she thought it would, admitting it to herself.

Now she had to say something to Johnny, and to the others in school and to the administration. She had the tool, her writing, and the power to write it the way it would be understood. She would make them understand what Johnny and she would need so that they didn't feel disabled. Then she would deal with the marathon committee.

Sam sat at the desk for hours, framing one word after the other, painting verbal pictures of anger, then desperation, none of them quite fitting the way she wanted them to fit, the pile of crumpled paper piling higher and higher next to her desk.

Mandy began to play with them, rolling them around the bedroom and tossing them high into the air.

Then, as often happened, for no particular reason, simple words slid across the paper, as if they had been hiding, playing games, and suddenly decided to come out and play. There they were, easily taking their proper places, building and building until Sam could feel the excitement in her fingertips.

She reread the finished product.

See Jane. She is in a wheelchair!

See Dick. Over there. He is in a wheel-chair, too!

Dick and Jane travel sitting down. That is really the only difference between them and you. You travel standing up, except when you are in a car. Then you, too, are sitting down.

Dick and Jane like to do many things.

They like to shop in stores.

Sometimes they can't get in (steps, narrow doorways).

They like to eat in restaurants.

Sometimes they can't get in (steps, narrow doorways).

They like to go to school.

Sometimes they can't get in (steps, narrow doorways).

They like to use school bathrooms.

Sometimes they can't get in (steps, narrow doorways).

Dick tried to make the bathrooms wider so that they could get in.

He got expelled.

Now Jane is sad. Dick is sad.

Help Dick get back in school.

Help Dick and Jane get in the toilets.

Walk out at 12:00 today.

Walk out so Dick and Jane can get in.

The words were brazenly set before her. Did she dare take such an extreme step? She hadn't

known it would come out like that, that she
would ask such a thing of her fellow students. Yet
she knew she needed their commitment if anything was to get done. Wasn't their goal worth this
step? Johnny and she had to know if there was
anyone out there who would support them. The
principal had done what he had to do. She didn't
blame him for that. But the issue remained unre-
solved. Was it just the two of them now fighting
the windmills?

Sam wheeled out into the living room. There
was a matter she had to settle first. Her father was
napping. His head lay back on the top of the sofa,
contentedly. He sensed her being there, and
opened his eyes. He had a way of sensing many
things about her. She handed him the paper.

"They won't let me compete in the marathon."
Her father had become part of her early-morning
runs by getting up a little earlier to share the
dawn excitement of her going out to train. She
saw the hurt in his eyes. It was odd how the pain
of being rejected was beginning to spread, like a
contagious disease, touching those she loved.

"I can't accept their answer. I won't. Just like
Johnny couldn't accept the attitude of the school.
Do you understand that, Dad? Johnny and I are in
this together. I have to help him now, so that he
can help me. We need to help each other."

Her father read the fiery words on the paper.
Then he looked up at her. Quietly, he put the pa-
per down on the table and went to the hall closet.
He took down his winter coat and put it on.

"Where are you going? Sam asked, worried at his reaction.

"You'll need copies of these to hand out tomorrow, won't you? I'll run over to the photocopying place, get him to make up a couple of hundred copies. That should be enough, shouldn't it?"

"Papa," she said, and took hold of his hand. She hadn't called him Papa since she was a little girl and she had looked up to him like some brave warrior. Sam felt he was that now . . . a warrior who would join her battle, no matter what the cost.

She fell asleep that night before he returned, but the stack of papers on her desk the following morning was all the support she needed.

She and Mandy hurried to school, rushing her mother while the papers sat comfortably in her lap, a passkey to Johnny's freedom.

Samantha began to pass out the papers during her first class. She gave a couple of stacks to some students from different grades as they passed her in the halls. Recognizing some of Johnny's friends, she asked them to help in getting the word around.

She wasn't sure what the response would be. Though many had stood in the halls watching and encouraging them, this was a different matter. This was a commitment and people didn't take to commitments that easily. Moral support was one thing, a walkout was another.

Each time she passed the toilets she still could see the shadows of signs and Johnny's face, the

NOD members, the dogs sitting quietly. They seemed to be there still, hiding in the corners, not letting her forget. They gave her strength.

Moment by moment, whenever she could, during, after, and in between class, she pushed the pieces of paper into curious hands, and always, she added, "Please tell others, spread the word around."

It was 11:30 when she got to Sue Jenkins's room. The class had just left. Sue had called her last night with a concerned, "What are we going to do now, Sam?" She looked toward her for the answer.

Sam had just said, "I'll tell you tomorrow."

Now she was here to deliver the answer. "Here, Ms. Jenkins." She still called her that, though the months had sewn them closer together in friendship than Sam had ever had with a girl her own age. Still, in school, she gave her that show of respect that she knew was so important to her as a teacher. Samantha slid the paper across the desk and wheeled back toward the door.

"I don't expect you to come," she said. "I don't want you to get into trouble. I just wanted you to know what's going on, and that I'm not finished when it comes to the marathon."

At 11:45, Sam put on her coat and, with Mandy at her side, went out into the cold March winds.

Sam wheeled down the driveway. She looked back at the long, rectangular school with its tiny windows. The lights were all on to erase the March gloominess.

She sat there with Mandy, wishing that Johnny

were with her, understanding now how alone he must have felt, how one more wheelchair could have made such a big difference.

She glanced at her watch: 11:55. Had she been a dreamer? Was it too much to expect that anyone would understand or care to fight for something that didn't involve him or her personally, something as remote as a bathroom?

At 12:00, there was a moment when Samantha felt decisions were being made in each of the classrooms. In that moment she dared not think of the outcome.

A tiny trickle of students started streaming from a side door about 12:05, and then another side door opened with more students coming out. Then the front door, and from around the back. Slowly, the front grounds filled up with coated classmates. Some sat on the cold ground. Others stood huddled by trees.

Someone had salvaged one of Johnny's signs and now it stood proudly once again, leaning against a tree at the top of the slope, propped up over heads so that everyone could see it.

Sam looked around her. It was as if the entire school were outside on the front lawn. Someone passed around a container of hot chocolate.

"Oh, Johnny," she whispered, "how I wish you were here to see this."

She sat there, part of the crowd, unable to see above the top of anyone's head. Two boys came up from behind and pushed her up the slope, next to Johnny's sign on top of the hill.

Mandy ran at their heels, barking a warning not to wheel Sam out of her sight.

"It's your game now, Sam," said one of the boys. "You should be where everyone can see you."

She sat there looking down on the faces that were turned her way.

"We're with you, Sam." She heard the shouts. She saw the hands wave. "You and Johnny, we're with you both."

Samantha didn't realize she was capable of feeling so much love and caring all at once. It overwhelmed her. It reached out from the crowd in front of her and held her tightly.

A car with a *Daily Record* newspaper sign attached to its roof pulled up in the driveway. Two men made their way through the crowd to where Sam was sitting.

"Are you Samantha Lee Anderson?"

"Yes."

"We received a call tipping us off that there's been a walkout going on here." He gave the hill a sweeping look. The man next to him focused his camera.

"Do you mind letting us in on what this is all about?"

Samantha handed him a paper. She told the reporter about the toilets, the 504 bill, and Johnny. Johnny was between every other word as she tried to explain the urgency of their situation.

Sam filled him in on the past months, on Johnny's daily crusade, on the demonstrations, on the confusion surrounding the toilet alterations.

The reporter's pen sped across the pages of his notebook.

"So it all comes down to the use of the toilets?"

"Yes, that's the issue," Sam agreed. "It might seem like a small issue, but only if you can use them. Sure, someone could carry us, but then we risk the danger of being dropped. And to go home, or not to be able to attend a certain school or college, to be deprived of an education because of a door that isn't wide enough . . ."

The reporter continued taking notes as he mixed through the crowd.

"How long are you going to stay out here?" He came back to Sam.

"I don't know about them, but I'll stay as long as I have to." A sense of power swept over Samantha. Even if the crowd before her left, she wasn't afraid to stay alone. Even her single action would stand as a reminder of Johnny and what he had attempted to do.

She remembered in history class learning of the importance of the action of one human being . . . one man killed the heir to the throne of Austria and started the First World War . . . one man researching in a laboratory found the answer to a polio epidemic and eradicated the disease. Why not one girl . . . in a wheelchair?

The reporter shook his head. His question brought her back. "Do you think you'll win?"

"I'm not winning," Sam said sharply, "they are." She pointed to the school. "It's everyone's victory."

The hill grew empty at five. The sun went down. The sky grew dark.

The officials looking out from the inside of the school breathed a joint sigh of relief. It was over. At last the day was over. They had toughed it out. There had been no violence, no incidents. The students had left cold and hungry and probably discouraged. The administration had played it right. In a week it would all be forgotten.

What they didn't count on was the next morning, when, bright and early, almost rising with the sun, the front of the school yard again filled up with students. Samantha and Mandy sat quietly on the slope, beside Johnny's sign. The classes inside the school remained empty.

The school officials thought it was over, when actually it had just begun.

9 ———

Samantha lay back on the tiny green shoots just finding their way out into the spring sunlight. Mandy rested next to her, her nose buried in the grass, sniffing for possible treasures buried underneath. Lying there, it was almost hard to believe that she was still on the roller coaster of the past month.

The demonstration in front of the school had lasted three days. The newspapers had put it on the front page, with editorials pressing the school board to action. On the third day, Johnny had come to the school to take his place with them. Samantha lay there, feeling again the warmth that came from the school grounds, the day of the walkout, even though the March winds had howled their warnings. The light had burned brightly inside the school, late into the night, as teachers met with principals and board members met with parents, and around and around it went.

Each day the reporters would come out and get another interview, another viewpoint. Each day the story would be spread over the newspapers.

At the end of the third day, the answer had come, very quietly. The principal of the school had walked out of the building and, unnoticed in the oncoming twilight of the day, made his way through the crowd until he reached Samantha and Johnny. "We'd like to meet with you both inside," he said.

At the meeting was a NOD consultant. The school admitted its financial problems. The principal gave the group an idea of just how much money he had to work with. The NOD consultant, using the minimal amount of funds needed, explained how a door could be widened and a cubicle widened inside the toilet for just a couple of hundred dollars. It was much less than anyone in the administration had anticipated. Relief flooded the meeting. Everyone had assumed they were talking about thousands of dollars in alterations, when actually it could be done for very little. Just a doorway and a cubicle. The following week, a truck pulled up at the school. Work on the toilets began.

But there wasn't even a day to rest and forget. Samantha told Johnny about her application being turned down, and from then on it was back up and down the roller coaster. A phone call to NOD. A letter from NOD to the township. Another letter to the editor of the local newspaper from NOD. The letters all had the same theme. There were many marathons going on all over the country now taking in the physically disabled.

A private meeting followed with the NOD president, the committee running the marathon, Samantha, Sue Jenkins, and Johnny. Articles were strewn about the table showing how different marathons were handling disabled entries.

Someone suggested that the disabled have their own marathon.

It was turned down. "We don't always have to be separated," Johnny said defensively. "A marathon is a marathon. No one ever stated that you had to use your legs to compete in it."

And then came the compromise. Samantha's application was accepted on the condition that she begin the marathon fifteen minutes earlier, so that there would be no danger of injury to herself or anyone else at the finish line.

Samantha had eagerly agreed. She felt it was a fair decision. At the starting line, there would be confusion and tension, all releasing at one time. She and the wheelchair could possibly get in the way of the runners starting off at the same time. She could understand their wanting that protection for themselves as well as for herself.

Here she was now, the day before the marathon, and it was all crashing down upon her. The trees around her were trying to show off their early April leaves. The winds were still crisp, but the weather report for tomorrow had said warm.

In fact hot, with an unusual rise into the upper seventies. It occurred to her that it would be warm, sweaty warm, and it would be harder because of the heat. And then as that thought crept in, so had the other thoughts, the thought that yes, she was the only person in a wheelchair competing, and then, wondering how it had happened, how she had to come to want it so and fight for it, and then she pictured the crowds and thought of the twenty-six-mile stretch that would take her three hours, maybe more, in the heat. What if she couldn't or didn't make it? Her heart began to pound. Samantha knew fear of the marathon for the first time. Doubt crept in.

Maybe she hadn't done enough practice. Maybe she just wasn't good enough. Her arms had grown strong during the winter, and her endurance long. But the weather had been cold. No pressure. No spectators.

Tomorrow, the whole town would be there. After all the newspaper publicity, half the people would come out of curiosity. Wasn't she the girl who had spent three days in a wheelchair at the head of a demonstration? Here she was again, fighting for the chance to compete in the marathon. Who was this crusader she had become?

Johnny's car pulled up. Mandy jumped up to greet him, then parked herself under the shade of a nearby tree. Johnny joined them on the lawn.

"What's up, Sam?"

"My stomach."

"You have the jitters."

"I'm scared to death." She put her hand on his. It shook even lying there.

"I'm scared, too," he said.

"You are . . . of what?"

"Of you," he answered, half joking. Only his eyes were serious. "I've never felt lonely without someone. I mean my parents and the kid, Karon, but outside of them, I've never needed anyone that much. Know what I mean? But when you're not around lately, I feel lonely. That gets me scared, Sam."

The guy who demonstrated and faced police and principals unafraid looked toward her, uncertain.

She felt alone without him, too. He kissed her before he left. "It doesn't matter how you make out on Heartbreak Hill tomorrow," he said. "It doesn't matter to me if you're first, or last, or don't make it at all." He kissed her again. "It won't change how I feel this minute."

She looked at him, at his loving brown eyes. "It matters to me," she said firmly. "It's between me and the hill now."

On Saturday morning at 11:30 A.M., Samantha sat at the starting line. She wore light blue sweat trousers and a white T-shirt. The day, as promised, was warm and sunny. Her hair was pulled back and tucked under. She wore a sun visor to protect her eyes. She wore gloves on her hands to protect them against the vigorous strokes to her wheelchair. She had placed adhesive tape on parts of her fingers to protect the blisters that had already formed from the many hours of training. A water bottle was hooked up to the side of her chair.

The bearings and spokes had been checked on her wheelchair. Her hand rims were on tight.

The crowds had gathered and were lining the streets. Samantha could see Johnny waving frantically her way, and her mother and father. It seemed as if the entire school had turned out with signs: Go all the way, Samantha. We're with you, Sam. Do it with the wheelchair.

Sue Jenkins came over to her. "Good luck," she said, grasping her hand. There was nothing more to say. Now it was up to Samantha. And Mandy, who stood beside her at attention, sensing they were in the middle of the stage.

"Mandy, honey, this is the big one for you. They're going to shoot a gun," she petted the dog, "and you're going to get scared, but I love you, Mandy, and I need you today. I want you to make the race with me. I'm scared, too, just like you when you hear a loud noise. But I'm going to put my fears behind me now. Mandy, we're going up Heartbreak Hill together, all the way." She stroked the dog, waiting for the shot that would set her off ahead of the others.

"Mandy, I need you now. Don't let me down." During the past months, Sam had hoped that her love had set Mandy's fears aside. The dog seemed less and less nervous when faced with traffic noises in the city. Thinking back over it now, they both had come a long way.

The gun went off. She felt Mandy's body tense, like a piece of steel beside her. "Don't leave me, Mandy," she spoke to her as she began to push forward, over the starting line. The crowds cheered and shouted, bringing crashing sounds through the air. Mandy hesitated for a moment, letting Sam get ahead of her. And then, as though she had crossed her own starting line, she took off in Sam's direction, catching up to her and staying with her.

Pace yourself. Don't use yourself up. Sam remembered Sue's words. Mandy and she passed the warehouses, the rail crossings, the familiar sights she had registered in her mind from the countless hours of training.

A boy sat on a car and shouted, "It's twelve fifteen." She had been going for fifteen minutes. Push . . . push . . . even strokes . . . alone . . . all alone. She felt the eyes of everyone around her. But more than that, she heard their shouts: "That's the way, Samantha."

Street after street, around corners, over the pavement which was getting warmer from the midafternoon sun. Where were the others? How many miles had she gone? Someone called out one o'clock. The streets had folded into one another. Beads of perspiration streamed down her forehead and over her cheeks. It's just a training session, she told herself. Sue Jenkins is just around the corner, and we're going for our usual training session and we'll go all the way this time, and that's the only thing that's different.

"Mandy, do you know what, Mandy, today we're both doing something we might never do again." She looked over at the golden-hued dog. Just having her company, knowing she would face the noises for Sam, the uproar that she feared so, gave Sam renewed strength. She heard some footsteps behind her and realized that there were now runners ahead and to her side. She looked for Sue but couldn't see her yet.

A runner turned toward Sam. "You're doing great. Keep it up." She felt it again, like a big arm around her, the others pulling for her. No matter what happened today, she would always have that.

Again there was Johnny's face. He was spraying her with a hose. The cool water felt like a spring rain. She licked it from her mouth.

Sue Jenkins passed by. "How you doing, love?"

Sam just nodded, her arms and shoulders feeling heavier. Police stood along the way, holding the crowds back. Some spectators held out slices of oranges and ice. Sam reached out for a moment and grabbed an ice cube. She sucked on it slowly.

A man with a beard stroked it thoughtfully as she went by. He smiled. It touched her and sent her on again.

There was a refreshment stand near the ten-mile mark. Somone handed her a cold drink. There was a bowl of water for Mandy. Mandy sat down for a moment. She looked as if she were wondering if it was worth it. Sam could see the indecision on her face. "Come on, Mandy, we have to go the whole route." Mandy got up slowly. One cool lick to the cheek gave her acceptance.

Sam was getting tired. It was now about the twelfth mile. She could feel a nagging pain across her shoulders and down her back. Her fingers were pasted to the sides of the chair. Each stroke drained her. The heat was taking its toll.

She sucked on a piece of orange another runner had passed to her. It wakened her senses. Someone raised a sign. This is the 16th mile.

Sixteen miles, Mandy. Ten miles to go. Ten miles. Then nine. She began to count them down. It wouldn't be so bad. Now just nine more miles. The greater part of the marathon was behind her.

But then she saw it, looming before her like a gigantic mountain, tall and straight and threatening. Taunting her, facing her, just as she felt herself weakening, looking down at her with a smile on its face.

Heartbreak Hill. She was perspiring profusely now. Her mouth was dry.

"I can't, Mandy, I can't. Where are we going to get the strength to climb that hill? I can't," and even as she said she couldn't, she felt a strange, kitelike feeling come over her, as if she were flying up over herself. It wasn't she who was pushing the chair. It must be someone else. She felt separated from her body.

No one was around her anymore. They were all ahead. Many had dropped out already. Sam remained close to Mandy's side. She heard the crowd's hysterical chants around her. "You can do it, Sam. Just over the hill. The finish is on the other side."

She hated the hill. In that moment it stood for everything that had been in her way for so long, with everything possible on the other side. It stood for the toilets and the months of controlling her needs, and for the rejection from the marathon committee. It stood for the datelessness before she met Johnny and the doubt from the moment she had taken her place in the wheelchair. It stood for the stares and the obstacles, and everything she had never dared to cry out against before. There it was. All neatly packaged and tied together in front of her. And it was called Heartbreak Hill.

If she could beat it, she could beat anything. She knew it. Nothing would ever stop her on the other side of the hill. Never again. Push, Sam, push. People weren't meant to propel their bodies with their arms. Sue Jenkins had been right about that. What was she anyway, an aircraft? How could she have thought she could endure this? They had their legs. She was pushing everything, wheelchair and body. With just her two arms.

The crowd kept going with her. They were in unison, chanting her up the hill. "Go, Sam, go." She moved to the rhythm of their chant. The pains now shot across her chest and down her arms. Her fingers felt as if there were pins in them. Each touch was agony. The wheels of her chair felt hot to her touch. The gloves were ripped. The metal of the chair burned into her hands.

"I bet you didn't count on this, Mandy, did you, girl? I bet when I took you out of that kennel you were thinking about a nice quiet home and a blanket by a fireplace. That will teach you, Mandy."

Mandy jumped up and licked the sweat off her forehead. Someone held out a towel. "Get it, Mandy," Sam ordered. Mandy ran over and brought the towel back to her. Sam kept it with her, wiping the strands of hair off her forehead and away from her eyes. The sun visor grew heavy. She threw it off. Her hair came unstrung and was hanging down over her shoulders. Her cheeks burned from the sun's reflection. She squinted. Her eyes, salted with perspiration, stung. Farther up the hill. The hill seemed to be stretching as she reached out to its peak.

The runners were dropping out now, one after the other, just near the top, off to the sides, being carried away, like little flies, parched, exhausted. The hill had wiped them away. It stood there now, much of it behind Samantha, just the peak ahead. The cracks had tipped her wheelchair, the bumpy pavement had pushed her about. It was using every bit of its power to prevent her from reaching the top.

"You think you're going to wipe us out, don't you, Hill? Just before the finish, you with your slopes and bends and potholes. You think you have all the power."

Just as she reached the top, and heard the roaring exuberance around her, something mysterious and unexpected happened to her. Her entire body was filled with a new gust of energy. It made her feel that she could run another twenty miles.

"We're at the top, Mandy. We did it. We did it." She didn't have time to look back. Ahead of her were competitors, still running, toward the finish.

"Mandy, it's just ahead, just a little more." She was looking for the first aid station that would tell her the end was near. Two miles to go, a sign shot up. How long had she been going?

The yellow line. The finish. She thought she saw it, but then it turned into a streak of sunlight glimmering across the street. Police were waving to her. An electricity was running through the crowds. Again the chant caught on contagiously, "Go, Sam, go." Was she moving? She thought she had stopped long ago, and yet the wheels were still turning and Mandy's panting was loud and clear. Sam knew they were moving, yet she had no sense of pushing the wheels. Her hands were still on the rims. But her fingers were numb. The pain was gone. A sense of nothingness came over her.

But then a sleek, straight yellow line was just yards away. Banners and confetti floated down through the air. Everyone seemed to be crowded near the finish . . . calling to her, though their voices could have been miles away. "Come on,

Sam, come on." They were standing there on the line, cupping their hands, bringing her forward. Johnny, her mother and dad, Sue Jenkins, Johnny's parents. . . . "It's too far, Mandy. I'll stop just for a moment to rest." She knew if she did, it would be over. She would never start those wheels again. She would quit just feet away from the finish. "Don't stop, Sam." The chant began. It carried her over the long yellow strip.

"Mandy, didn't we do it?" she gasped. The wheels had come to a stop. She felt the cool water going over her. The rims of her chair rested just over the finish.

Mandy was on her lap, her paws resting there, her face down, as if she wanted to hide from the rushing crowds that were whirling all about them, sweeping them in, covering them with hands, confetti still twirling through the air like a gentle spring snowstorm.

"You did it, Sam." She heard Johnny's voice. She felt his arms around her. Her eyes were wet. She didn't know whether it was from tears or sprays from the cool showers going off over their heads.

Sue Jenkins was screaming, jumping up and down like a little girl. "We did it. We beat the hill." Sam tried to unscramble her words which were running together with excitement. "Sam, do you realize, out of fifteen hundred only fifty made it?"

"How long have I been wheeling?" Sam heard

her own voice ask the question, but she still felt detached from herself.

"Four hours. You've been wheeling for four hours, Sam. Twenty-six miles."

She turned to Johnny, and though there were hundreds crowded around them, streamers and cotton candy and police and the school band now marching down the street and filling the air with its music, it was just the two of them sitting there, alone.

"I did it, Johnny. I finished," she said faintly. She was so tired. She rested her head on his shoulder. She was so very exhausted, she barely heard him when he moved the sign on his lap which read, **Better Busing for the Disabled in Our Community**, and whispered, "Samantha, baby, we've just begun."

About the Author

Harriet May Savitz lives with her husband and two children near Philadelphia, Pennsylvania. She grew up and attended school in New Jersey.

She is the author of four other novels, including THE LIONHEARTED and WAIT UNTIL TOMORROW, both in Signet paperback, several short stories, and a nonfiction book on wheelchair athletes. She is presently a member of the National Wheelchair Athletic Association and the Pennsylvania Wheelchair Athletic Association. Her many years of experience working with the disabled and with wheelchair sports teams has enabled her to write sensitively about the problems and frustrations encountered by the handicapped as they enter the mainstream of life.

RUN, DON'T WALK was presented on TV as an ABC After School Special.